The
Reed
Cutter

AND

Captain
Shigemoto's
Mother

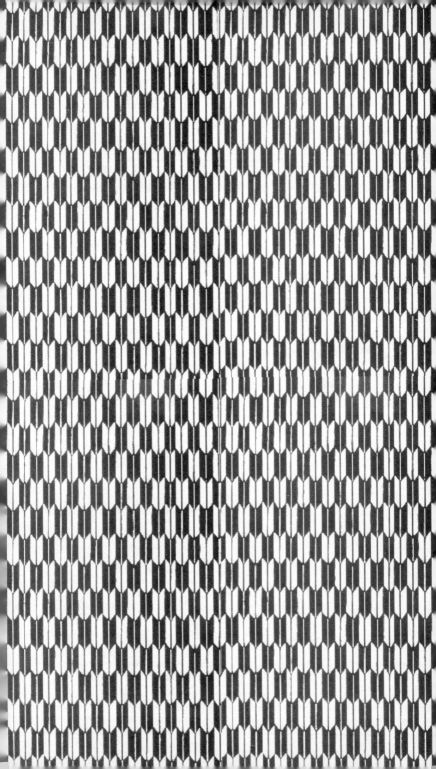

The
Reed
Cutter

AND

Captain
Shigemoto's
Mother

TWO NOVELLAS

Junichiro
Tanizaki

TRANSLATED FROM
THE JAPANESE BY
ANTHONY H. CHAMBERS

ALFRED A. KNOPF   NEW YORK   1994

Copyright © 1993 by Alfred A. Knopf, Inc.

These translations are based on the ChuoKoron-Sha, Inc., editions
of Ashikari, published in 1973, and Shōshō Shigemoto no Haha,
published in 1974, in Japan.

Library of Congress Cataloging-in-Publication Data
Tanizaki, Jun'ichirō, 1886–1965.
[Ashikari. English]
The reed cutter and Captain Shigemoto's mother: two novellas /
by Junichirō Tanizaki; translated from the Japanese by Anthony
H. Chambers.
p.   cm.
ISBN 0-679-42010-X
1. Tanizaki, Junichirō, 1886–1965—Translations into English.
I. Tanizaki, Jun'ichirō, 1886–1965.   Shōshō Shigemoto no haha.
English. 1994.   II. Title.   III. Title: Captain Shigemoto's mother.
PL839.A7A9413   1994
895.6'344—dc20   93-260   CIP

The
Reed
Cutter

How wretched I am without you, cutting reeds!
Life at Naniwa Bay grows harder still to bear.*

I T   H A P P E N E D one September when I was still living in Okamoto. The weather was splendid, and one evening—actually, a little past three o'clock—I felt a sudden urge to go out for a walk. The hour was too late for me to venture far, but I had already seen the sights nearby: there must, I thought, be some obscure, forgotten spot where I could take a stroll and still return home within two or three hours; and then I remembered Minase Shrine, where I had wanted to go but had not yet found the opportunity. Minase Shrine is on the site of the Detached Palace of Retired Emperor Gotoba. The first chapter of *The Larger Mirror*† describes the palace this way:

> His Majesty restored the Toba and Shirakawa Pal-
> aces and visited them constantly, but then he built

---

*Anonymous, *Shūiwakashū* (compiled early in the eleventh century) #540. "Ashikari," the original title of the novella, comes from this poem. The word denotes "reed cutting" and "reed cutter," and connotes "wretched," "miserable." Naniwa is an old name for Osaka.

†*Masukagami*, a fourteenth-century historical narrative. The Genkyū era began in the Second Month of 1204 and ended in the Fourth Month of 1206.

3

an indescribably delightful villa at a place called Minase, whither he often traveled for the blossoms and foliage of spring and fall and held entertainments to his heart's content, which were much talked about. The wide view over the river from the site was lovely indeed. In a contest for Chinese and Japanese poems that His Majesty held in the Genkyū era, one of the outstanding entries was:

> *Spring haze at the base of the mountain*
> *veils Minase River—*
> *Whatever made me think that evenings*
> *are best in fall?**

The thatched passageways that he had built were extensive, beautiful, and elegant. The placement of the rocks in a waterfall on the hill before the palace, the moss-covered trees on the mountain, and the interlacing branches of small pines in the garden truly made it a palace to flourish for a thousand ages. When His Majesty had completed the construction of the garden, he summoned many people for a concert, after which Middle Counselor Teika† (who was still of low rank then) presented these:

> *Standing here unaging through its first*
> *one thousand years,*
> *The young pine on the mountaintop*
> *pledges itself to my lord.*

---

*The tradition that evenings were best in autumn (and dawns in spring) is based on the early-eleventh-century *Pillow Book* of Sei Shōnagon.
†Fujiwara Teika, 1162–1241.

4

The waters diverted through the garden
in my lord's time
Course over a thousand boulders,
a thousand reigns.

Thus His Majesty came to spend much of his time at Minase Palace, accompanied by the sounds of koto and flute as he enjoyed entertainments of every kind in the seasons of blossoms and foliage.

The palace at Minase had been in the back of my mind ever since I read *The Larger Mirror* the first time, many years ago. I was fond of the Retired Emperor's poem: *"Spring haze at the base of the mountain veils Minase River— Whatever made me think that evenings are best in fall?"* Many of his other works—such as the poem on Akashi Bay, *"The fisherman's boat rowing into the mist,"* and *"I am the new guardian of the island,"* about Oki Island—appealed to me and lingered in my memory; but I yearned for the poignant, warm view over the upper waters of the Minase River that I pictured whenever I recited this particular poem. Before I was familiar with the geography of the Kansai region, I felt no urge to pinpoint the location, though I imagined that Minase was somewhere in the suburbs of Kyoto; only recently did I learn that the site of the palace is near the border of Yamashiro and Settsu provinces, on the Yodo River about two-thirds of a mile from the station at Yamazaki, and that a shrine dedicated to Retired Emperor Gotoba stands there even now. The time of day was just right to set out on a visit to the shrine at Minase. I could go directly to Yamazaki by steam train, but it would be even easier to take the Hankyū Electric Line and change to the New Keihan Line. What is more, the day corresponded to the fifteenth of the Eighth Month by the old calendar—on my way home I could enjoy the view of the full moon from the banks of the Yodo River.* With this plan in mind, I set out alone without announcing my destination—it was not the sort of place to invite women and children to.

Yamazaki is in Otokuni District, Yamashiro Province, and Minase in Mishima District, Settsu Province. When taking the New Keihan Line from Osaka to Ōyamazaki, one crosses the border between Settsu and Yamashiro, then crosses it again when backtracking to the site of the palace. I had been to Yamazaki only once before, when I strolled through the neighborhood around the National Line station; now for the first time I walked west along the Western Provinces Highway. After a little distance the road divides in two, and beside the right fork stands a weathered stone inscription, marking the road from Akutagawa to Itami by way of Ikeda. Recalling the battles of Araki Murashige and Ikeda Shōnyūsai as they are described in the *Nobunaga Chronicle,* I remembered that these generals of the Warring States Period had been active in a strip of territory along a line connecting Itami, Akutagawa, and Yamazaki. In the old days, then, this fork must have been the main road; the winding highway that I followed along the banks of the Yodo River would have been convenient for navigation but was probably unsuitable for overland travel because of the many bogs and inlets overgrown with reeds. For that mat-

---

*The Eighth Month fell in mid-autumn. The full moon of that month being considered the most beautiful of the year, it was customary to hold elaborate moon-viewing parties on the fifteenth, the night of the full moon.

ter, I had heard that the site of the Eguchi ferry was near the tracks that I had just ridden to come here. Today Eguchi is part of Greater Osaka, and Yamazaki has been absorbed into a metropolis with last year's expansion of Kyoto City, but because of its climate the area between Kyoto and Osaka has not gone the way of the region between Osaka and Kobe. Since it seems unlikely that "Pastoral Cities" and "Culture Subdivisions" will be developed here anytime soon, the area may retain the look of a grassy countryside for a little while yet. In the old days it must have been even more desolate than it is now—wild boars and robbers haunted the highway near here, according to *The Treasury of Loyal Retainers*;* but even today the thatched houses lining the road on both sides look terribly antiquated to an eye that is accustomed to the Westernized towns and villages along the Hankyū Line. Sugawara Michizane embraced Buddhism here on his way into exile— "Grieving that he was punished for no reason, he took the tonsure at Yamazaki," says *The Great Mirror*—and here he composed the famous poem that begins: *"The treetops where you live."*† This is, then, an extremely old post road. Yamazaki may well have been established as a relay station when the Heian capital was built. Mulling these thoughts over, I examined the houses one by one as I walked along the road. The air of the age of the shogun seemed to linger under their dark eaves.

(Kanadehon) Chūshingura, a popular eighteenth-century puppet and kabuki play.
†*Ōkagami*, a twelfth-century historical narrative, recounts the banishment of Sugawara Michizane (845–903) in 901 by his political rival, Fujiwara Shihei.

I crossed a bridge over what must have been the Minase River, walked a little farther, and then turned left off the highway to reach the site of the palace. A government-supported shrine stands there now, dedicated to Gotoba, Tsuchimikado, and Juntoku, the three emperors who met equally unhappy fates in the Jōkyū War,* but the shrine buildings and grounds are not especially noteworthy for a region rich in splendid shrines and Buddhist temples. Still, when I recalled the story that I quoted earlier from *The Larger Mirror* and thought of the early-Kamakura courtiers holding seasonal banquets on this very spot, I found myself moved by every tree and stone. I sat down beside the road and smoked a cigarette, then wandered around the grounds, which were not extensive. Though not far off the highway, the site occupied a cozy cul-de-sac, peaceful and obscure behind a scattering of farmhouses, autumn plants of every variety blossoming on their rough-woven fences. Retired Emperor Gotoba's palace would not have been confined to such a small area; it must have extended all the way to the bank of the Minase River, which I had passed a few minutes before. There, seated in a pavilion at the water's edge, or strolling in his garden, the Retired Emperor would have gazed upstream and expressed his excitement for the "spring haze at the base of the mountain veiling Minase River."

His Majesty went out one summer to the angling pavilion at Minase Palace, where he shared ice

---

*Court nobles rallying around Retired Emperor Gotoba failed in their attempt to overthrow the shogunate in 1221. Gotoba was exiled to Oki, Tsuchimikado and Juntoku to Sado.

water and cold rice porridge and other dishes with some young nobles and courtiers.* When the drinking began, he said, How wonderful was Murasaki Shikibu! Her *Tale of Genji* is truly splendid: his son and the others prepared trout for Genji from a nearby stream, and bass from the Katsura River. I wonder if anyone does that kind of cooking today? A bodyguard named Hata, on duty nearby at the foot of the balustrade, overheard His Majesty. He rinsed some white rice in cold water, scattered the grains on a few leaves of bamboo grass that he had taken from the edge of the lake, and presented them to the Retired Emperor. I see!—It will melt when it is lifted!† This, too, is not a bad effort, said His Majesty, removing one of his robes and giving it to the man. He often held such drinking parties.

Considering this passage in relation to the setting, I guessed that the lake beside the angling pavilion must have connected with the Minase. And to the south, probably several hundred yards behind the shrine, flows the Yodo

---

*Gotoba is deliberately re-creating the scene at the beginning of "Wild Carnations" *(Tokonatsu)*. See Murasaki Shikibu, *The Tale of Genji*, translated by Edward Seidensticker (Knopf, 1976), p. 441. In the original *Genji*, the "wine and ice water and other refreshments" of Seidensticker's translation include the porridge that Gotoba eats here.

†The bodyguard and Gotoba allude to a passage in "The Broom Tree" *(Hahakigi)* chapter of *The Tale of Genji* (Seidensticker, p. 32: "the speck of frost will melt when it is lifted from the bamboo leaf").

River. The Yodo was out of sight, but the thickly wooded peak of Mount Otoko Hachiman on the far bank loomed so close at hand that it seemed about to fall on my brow, as though there were not a great river flowing between it and me. I gazed up at this shadowy mountain of Iwashimizu* and then at the peak of Mount Tennō, towering opposite it, to the north of the shrine. I had not noticed as I walked along the highway, but now, standing here and looking in all directions, I realized that the valley was like the base of a cauldron, the mountains to the north and south serving as folding screens to define the sky above. Studying the position of the mountains and rivers, I could easily understand why a barrier station had been established at Yamazaki during the age of the Heian court and why this was a strategic point for anyone on his way to invade Kyoto. The Yamashiro Plain around Kyoto to the east and the plain of Settsu, Kawachi, and Izumi provinces around Osaka to the west contracted here to a narrow passage, with a single great river flowing through it. Thus Kyoto and Osaka are linked by the Yodo River, but their climates and cultures differ, and this spot is the dividing line. Osakans say that the sky will sometimes be clear west of Yamazaki when it is raining in Kyoto, and that in winter one can feel the temperature drop as the train passes Yamazaki on its way to Kyoto. Come to think of it, the villages with their many bamboo groves, the design of the farmhouses, the shape of the trees, and the color of the soil recall the outskirts around Saga, and one feels that the Kyoto countryside extends to this point.

Leaving the shrine grounds, I followed a path beyond

*Mount Otoko is the site of the Iwashimizu Hachiman Shrine.

the highway back to the edge of the Minase River and climbed the embankment. The shape of the mountains upstream and the view of the waters have probably changed over the last seven hundred years, but the lovely scene now before my eyes was much the same as the image I had conceived from reading the Retired Emperor's poem. I had always thought the view would be like this. It was not a landscape that anyone would call a beauty spot or a scenic masterpiece, featuring craggy precipices or rapids that chewed at the boulders. Gentle hills and tranquil streams, softly veiled in the evening mist—it was a genial, refined, and peaceful scene, like those in old Japanese paintings.* Natural scenery will be viewed differently by different people, and there are probably some who would not consider a place like this worth a glance. But I am more apt to be lured into sweet daydreams by ordinary hills and streams like these, neither majestic nor unique, and find myself wanting to linger on and on. A scene like this one welcomes the traveler with a friendly smile, instead of startling the eye and enthralling the spirit. At a glance it would seem to be nothing, but standing here for a long time one is moved by a gentle affection, like the warm embrace of a loving mother. On a lonely evening, in particular, one longs to be drawn into those upstream mists, beckoning from afar. As Retired Emperor Gotoba said, Whatever made us think that evenings are best in the fall? If this were a spring evening, with a scarlet haze trailing at the foot of the graceful hills, and cherry trees in blossom here and

---

* *Yamato-e*, Heian and Kamakura period paintings on Japanese subjects, as opposed to *kara-e*, paintings in Chinese styles on Chinese subjects.

there on the riverbanks, on the peaks, and in the valleys, how much warmer still the setting would be! No doubt it was just such a scene that the Retired Emperor viewed. But true elegance can be understood only by city dwellers with the most refined taste; were it not for the courtiers' aesthetic sensibilities, this scene of elegance in mediocrity might well have been dismissed as dull. Standing atop the embankment as the evening darkened around me, I turned my eyes downstream. Searching for the site of the angling pavilion in which the Retired Emperor ate chilled porridge with his senior nobles and courtiers, I surveyed the right bank and saw that it was covered with a luxuriant forest that extended all the way to the rear of the shrine. I could see that the entire broad area of the forest had been the site of the detached palace. From here the great Yodo River was visible, and the Minase flowing into it. All at once the strategic position of the detached palace came clear to me. The palace must have faced on the Yodo to the south and on the Minase to the east, and embraced a magnificent garden of many acres in the corner of land formed by their confluence. In that case, yes, the Retired Emperor could have come down by boat from Fushimi and moored below the balustrade of the angling pavilion, and he could have traveled freely between here and the capital. This is consistent with the text of *The Larger Mirror*, which says that His Majesty came to spend much of his time at Minase Palace. I recalled the plutocrats' elegant villas that stood on the banks of the Sumida River at Hashiba, Imado, Komatsujima, and Kototoi during my childhood.* Perhaps this is an impertinent comparison, but when the Retired Emperor

*Hashiba, Imado, Komatsujima, and Kototoi are in Tokyo.

held elegant banquets at his palace here, and said, "How wonderful was Murasaki Shikibu! I wonder if anyone does that kind of cooking today?" or "I see!—It will melt when it is lifted! This, too, is not a bad effort," and rewarded his attendant with a gift, am I alone in thinking there was something about his manner that resembles the Edo sophisticate? The Sumida River is insipid, but the view of the great Yodo—with boats passing upstream and down in the shadow of Mount Otoko's green slopes—must have comforted the Retired Emperor and added to the pleasure that he took in his palace. Later, when the plot to overthrow the shogunate had been quashed and he spent nineteen sad years on Oki Island, listening to the wind and the waves and recalling his past glory, it must have been the shape of these hills and the color of these waters and the many gorgeous entertainments he held at this palace that came most often to his mind. While I was lost in these reflections, my daydreams wandered here and there, sketching visions of those times, and deep in my ears I could hear the lingering tones of the strings and winds, the murmur of the waters on the lake, and finally even the happy voices of the nobles and courtiers. Then I realized that dusk was close at hand, and when I took out my watch it was already six o'clock. The day had been warm enough that walking left me covered with perspiration, but when the sun went down, the autumn breeze was cold against my skin. Suddenly I was hungry. I would need to dine someplace while I waited for the moon to rise. Leaving the embankment, I returned to the highway.

I knew this was not the sort of town to have a smart restaurant—it would be enough just to warm myself for a time, and so when I came upon the lights of a noodle shop,

I went in, drank about a pint of saké, and ate two bowls of fox noodles. Before I left I had the proprietor heat a bottle of Masamune saké. Taking it with me, I descended toward the riverbed along a road that led, according to the proprietor, to a ferry landing. When I told him that I wanted to take a boat onto the Yodo River to view the moon, he said, In that case, right at the edge of this town is a ferry to Hashimoto on the opposite shore. We call it a ferry, but the river's wide and there's a sandbar in the middle. You cross from this side to the sandbar first, change to another boat, and go on to the other side, and during the crossing you can enjoy the view of the river. There's a pleasure district in Hashimoto, he added, right where the ferryboat docks, and so the ferry runs until ten or eleven at night. If you like, you can go back and forth any number of times and enjoy the view at your leisure. Grateful for his kindness, I started on my way, feeling the cool night breeze on my flushed cheeks as I walked. The road seemed longer than the proprietor had said, but when I reached the ferry landing I saw that indeed there was a sandbar in the river. I could make out the downstream tip of the bar just in front of me, but upstream the bar disappeared in the vast dim light and seemed to extend forever. The bar might not have been an island in the middle of the great river but a point of land formed by the confluence of the Katsura and the Yodo rivers. In any case, the Kizu, Uji, Kamo, and Katsura rivers all come together nearby, and here converge the waters of five provinces—Yamashiro, Ōmi, Kawachi, Iga, and Tamba. An old illustrated book called *A View of the Banks of the Yodo River* reports that there was a ferry landing called Fox Crossing a little upstream from here, where the river was 660 feet across. Probably it was even wider here. The sandbar is not in the middle of the river but much closer to this bank. As I sat waiting on the riverbed gravel, I watched the ferryboat set out from the flickering lights of Hashimoto on the far shore and row to the bar. The passengers disembarked and walked toward me across the bar to the water's edge, where another boat awaited them. It occurred to me that I had not taken a ferry ride in many years, but compared to those I remember from my childhood, at Sanya, Takeya, Futago, and Yaguchi,* this one had an easygoing elegance, interrupted as it was by the sandbar. Surprised that such an old-fashioned means of transport remained nowadays between Kyoto and Osaka, I congratulated myself on making a rare find.

The picture of Hashimoto in *A View of The Banks of the Yodo River,* the book I mentioned before, shows the moon suspended in the sky behind Mount Otoko. Accompanying it are a *waka* by Kageki: *"Mount Otoko: in the light of the moon rising from behind the peak, they come into view all around, the Yodo riverboats;"* and a haiku by Kikaku: *"Full moon! When was Mount Otoko ever old?"*† As the ferryboat rowed up to the sandbar, Mount Otoko loomed darkly in the sky, which retained a trace of evening glow. On its back the mountain bore a perfectly round moon, just as in the illustration, and the luxuriant growth of trees had the texture of velvet. When the ferryman invited me to board the boat on the other side of the bar, I said I'll board later, but I want to enjoy the river breeze here for a while. I tramped alone through dewy grasses to the tip of the sandbar and crouched among the reeds at the shore. From here I could

*These places, too, are in the Tokyo area.
†Kagawa Kageki, 1768–1843; Enomoto Kikaku, 1661–1707.

enjoy a full view of both riverbanks as they extended in the
moonlight, just as if I were riding a boat in midstream. The
moon was to my left as I faced downstream. The river,
wrapped now in a romantic blue light, looked even broader
than it had under the evening light a few minutes before.
Mellifluous phrases from Chinese works I had not thought
of for many years—Tu Fu's poem on Lake T'ung-t'ing,
lines from *The Lute Song,* and part of *The Red Cliff*—rose
sonorously to my lips.* Come to think of it, many boats
would have been sailing to and fro on an evening like this
in the old days, as in Kageki's "they come into view all
around, the Yodo riverboats," but now there was nothing
resembling a boat at all, except the occasional ferry with its
five or six passengers. Drinking straight from the bottle of
Masamune I had brought with me, I gave myself over to
the effects of the saké and sang, " 'At night by the river at
Hsun Yang I send off my guest; maple leaves and bush-
clover blossoms sigh in the wind.' " As I sang, it occurred
to me that the scene of Po Chü-i's *Lute Song* must have been
enacted many times here, too, near these thickly growing
reeds.† Since Eguchi and Kanzaki were not far downstream
from here, not a few courtesans must have cruised this area,
poling their little boats through the reeds. In the preface to
his poem "On Seeing Courtesans," the Heian scholar
Ōe-no-Masahira describes the prosperity and laments the
licentiousness of these shores:

*The poets are Tu Fu (712–770; "Climbing Yüeh-yang Pavilion");
Po Chü-i (772–846); and Su Shih (or Su Tung-p'o, 1037–1101).
†*The Lute Song* concerns a former courtesan from the capital
whom the poet has seen on a boat, accompanying herself on the
lute as she sings the story of her life.

The North Bank lies at the boundary of three provinces, Yamashiro, Kawachi, and Settsu, and is one of the most important harbors in the land. Anyone traveling in either direction, from west, east, south, or north, must pass this way. It is the custom in this place for women young and old to offer their sexual favors openly for sale. Spying a village, they moor their boats at the gates and wait on the river for guests. The young ones lead men astray with rouge, white powder, and songs; the old ones make it their responsibility to carry umbrellas and hold the poles. . . . Oh! They say the decorum behind emerald curtains in a crimson bedchamber is different in every way, but a life of pleasure parties taken in boats on the waves comes to the same thing. Always when I pass this way I heave a long sigh for what I see.

In a book called *An Account of Courtesans*, Masahira's descendant Ōe-no-Masafusa also describes the lively and voluptuous customs along these shores:*

Villages dot the north and south banks. At a fork in the river as it enters the province of Kawachi is a place called Eguchi. Here are the manors Ajiwaraki of the Bureau of Medicine and Ōba of the Bureau of Housekeeping. Farther downstream, in the province of Settsu, there are places called Kanzaki and Kanishima. The streets are lined with gates and houses. Groups of song girls

*Masahira, 952–1012; Masafusa, his great-grandson, 1041–IIII.

pole out in little boats to examine ships on the river and invite the men to share their pillows and quilts. Their voices rise beyond the clouds over the river, the echoes linger in the breeze across the water; and every traveler forgets his home. . . . Fishermen and traders line up their ships prow to rudder, so that there seems to be no water. Surely this is the most carefree place in the world.

While I searched through hazy memories for fragments of these texts, I gazed at the lonely surface of the water flowing silently under the clear light of the moon. I suppose everyone thinks fondly of the past. But as I approach fifty years of age, the sadness of autumn presses in upon me with a mysterious force that I could not have imagined in my youth; there is no shaking off the poignancy of seeing the arrowroot leaves rustle in the wind; and crouching in a place like this on an evening like this, I sigh all the more for the transience of humanity, whose endeavors fade without a trace, and my longing deepens for the gay world of the past. Famous courtesans named Kannon, Nyoi, Censer, and Peacock are mentioned in *An Account of Courtesans*. The names of others have come down to us as well—Little Kannon, Yakushi, Yuya, and Naruto. Where have these floating women gone? It is said that they took professional names redolent of Buddhism in a belief that selling sexual pleasure was the act of a bodhisattva. Would it be impossible to raise them to the surface of this stream for a time, like bubbles forming on the water—these women who likened themselves to avatars of Samantabhadra and were even revered by a venerable sage?

Courtesans' houses crowd the north and south banks of the river at Eguchi and Katsuramoto. These women give their hearts over to travelers' desires, and when their empty lives, spent in frivolous deeds, come to an end, what will their next life be? Perhaps their fate is the result of having been courtesans in a former life. Saying that they wish to prolong their dewlike existence, they perform acts that the Buddha has strictly forbidden. Their own transgressions are bad enough, and is it not still more disgraceful that they lead countless others into error? Yet many courtesans have been reborn in the Pure Land; some who dwelt among fishermen who kill living things were especially meritorious.

Perhaps, as Saigyō has written, these women have been reborn in Amida's paradise, where they smile with pity that what never changes in any age is the wretchedness of humanity.*

As I sat alone pursuing these thoughts, one or two verses began to take shape in my mind. Lest I forget them, I took out my notebook and began to write with a pencil in the moonlight. Feeling a lingering desire for the remaining saké, I took a swallow and wrote, took another swallow and wrote some more, and when I had extracted the last drop I flung the bottle onto the surface of the river. Just then there was a rustling in the reeds nearby, and when I turned to look, a man was squatting there like

*Saigyō (1118–1190), the celebrated poet-priest, is the "venerable sage" mentioned earlier.

me among the reeds, as if he were my shadow. I stared at him rudely for a moment, having been taken by surprise, but he did not flinch. It's a splendid moon, isn't it, he greeted me in a resonant voice. What fine taste you have. To tell the truth, I've been here for some time, though I restrained myself for fear of disturbing your elegant mood, and hearing you sing *The Lute Song,* I felt like humming a bit of something myself. I'm sorry to impose on you, but perhaps you'd be kind enough to listen for a moment, he said. For a stranger to speak up so familiarly is almost unheard of in Tokyo, but of late I had not only ceased to question the frankness of Kansai people, I had adapted to local ways. You are most courteous, I said smoothly. By all means, let me hear you sing. Rising quickly, he pushed through the rustling reeds and sat beside me. Excuse me, but won't you have a sip? he said, unwrapping something that had been bound with a string to his natural-wood staff. In his left hand he held a gourd, and with his right he offered me a lacquered saké cup. A moment ago you threw your bottle away, but I still have this much, he said, shaking the gourd. Please accept this in exchange for listening to my clumsy singing. If you sober up now it will dampen your pleasure. You needn't worry about drinking a little too much, since the breeze off the river here is cold. Forcing me to take the cup, he filled it. The saké made a pleasing gurgle as it came out of the gourd. Thank you; then I shall have some, I said. I drained the cup. What brand it was I do not know, but after the bottled Masamune, this mellow, chilled saké, subtly fragrant from the wooden cask, instantly refreshed my mouth. Here, please have another . . . and another, he said, quickly refilling my cup twice, and as I drank the third cupful he began slowly to sing *Kogō*.* He was short of breath and seemed to be laboring—perhaps he had drunk a little too much. His voice lacked volume and could not have been described as beautiful, but it was a practiced voice, charged with an austere elegance. His poise suggested that he had been practicing for many years. More than anything else, though, his spirit of serene detachment possessed me as I listened to him sing unself-consciously before a total stranger and saw how he immersed himself at once in the world of the song, untroubled by mundane thoughts. It occurred to me that the study of polite accomplishments is not pointless, even if one fails to master the technique, if it enables one to nurture this state of mind. That was splendid, I said. Thanks to you, I feel refreshed. Gasping for breath, he wetted his mouth, then held the cup out to me. Please have another, he said. He wore a hunting cap pulled down over his forehead. The visor cast a shadow over his face, so that it was difficult to make out his features in the moonlight; but he seemed to be about my age, and on his small, slender body he wore an everyday kimono with a traveling coat. Have you come from Osaka? I asked, noting his west-of-Kyoto accent. Yes; I have a little shop in the south of Osaka, where I deal in antiques, he said. And are you on your way home from a walk? No, no, I came out this evening to view the moon. Usually I take the Keihan Electric Line, but this year I had the good fortune to come a roundabout way, ride the New Keihan, and make this

*A nō play by Komparu Zenchiku (1405–1468). In the best-known section, a messenger searches for the emperor's beloved Kogō under a full moon in Sagano, on the western edge of Kyoto. He finds her by following the sound of her koto.

crossing. As he spoke he pulled a smoking case from his sash and filled a pipe with shredded tobacco. Do you mean that you choose someplace to go moon-viewing every year? Yes, he said. He was silent for a moment while he lit his tobacco. Every year I go moon-viewing at Lake Ogura, but I'm glad that I chanced to pass this way tonight and could see the moon here in the middle of the river. I'm indebted to you, because, you see, it was only when I noticed you relaxing here that I realized what a good spot this is. The moon is extraordinary, isn't it, viewed through the reeds, with the waters of the Yodo on either side? Emptying the embers onto a netsuke, he used them to light a fresh batch of tobacco and said, Perhaps you've come up with some good verses and would let me hear them? Oh, no, they're embarrassingly bad, not the sort of thing I'd want you to hear. I quickly put away my notebook. You mustn't be so modest, he said, though he did not press me, and then, as if he had forgotten all about it, he calmly chanted, " 'The moon glows on the river, wind rustles in the pines; what is the reason for this long, clear night?' "* By the way, I said, if you're from Osaka, you must be familiar with the geography and history of this area. Do you suppose that courtesans like the Lady of Eguchi poled their boats around this sandbar? That, more than anything else, is what I see as I look at the moon—visions of those women floating dimly before my eyes. I was trying to put my feelings into a poem as I pursued these visions, but it wouldn't take shape as I wished. Then everyone has similar thoughts, said the man. He appeared to be deeply moved.

*Lines by the T'ang poet-priest Hsüan Chüeh (also known as Yung-chia Ta-shih).

I was just thinking the same thing, he said with feeling. I, too, was sketching visions of the past as I viewed this moon. You appear to be about my age, I said, peering into his face. It's a factor of our age, is it not? This year more than last, last year more than the year before—with every passing year my sense grows stronger of a loneliness, a dreariness in autumn, a seasonal sadness that comes from nowhere, for no reason. "The sound of the wind awakens me"; "Stirring the blinds at my door, the autumn wind blows"—it's only after we've reached this age that we come to understand the true flavor of these old poems.* But this doesn't mean that I hate the autumn because it's sad. In my youth I liked the spring best of all, but now I look forward more to autumn. As we grow older we come to a sort of resignation, a state of mind that lets us enjoy our decline in accordance with the laws of nature, and we come to wish for a quiet, balanced life, do we not? And so we derive more comfort from a lonely scene than from a gorgeous view, and we find it more fitting to lose ourselves in memories of past pleasures than to indulge in real pleasure. In other words, for a young person, love for the past is nothing but a daydream unrelated to the present, but an older person has no other means for living through the present. The man nodded vigorously. Yes, yes, it's just as you say. I suppose it's natural for an ordinary person to get that way with age, but

---

*Fujiwara Toshiyuki, *Kokinshū* 169:

> *With my eyes I cannot clearly see that autumn has come,*
> *But the sound of the wind awakens me.*

Princess Nukada, *Man'yōshū* 488:

> *As I await you I pine for love—*
> *Stirring the blinds at my door, the autumn wind blows.*

even when I was a child my father took me every year, on the evening of the Fifteenth Night festival, for a walk of five miles or more under the moon, and those days come back to me on the Fifteenth Night. Come to think of it, my father said what you have just said: You probably won't understand the sadness of this autumn night, he often told me, but a time will come when you do understand. What's that you say? Did your father love the moon of the Fifteenth Night that much? And why did he take you on a walk of five miles or more when you were still a small child? Well, I was six or seven the first time he took me along. I didn't understand what we were doing. My father and I lived alone in a little house on an alley, my mother having died two or three years before, and so I suppose he couldn't go out without me. My boy, he'd say, I'll take you moon-viewing, and we'd leave the house while it was still light outside. There were no electric trains in those days; I remember boarding a steamboat at Hachikenya and sailing up this river. We got off at Fushimi, but at first I didn't know that it was Fushimi. Father would simply walk along the top of an embankment, on and on, and I'd follow him until we came to a lake. Now I know that the embankment was the Ogura Embankment and the lake was Lake Ogura.* The distance would have been four or five miles in each direction. But—I interrupted—why did you go there to walk? Did you just stroll around looking at the moon reflected in the lake? Yes; Father would sometimes stop on the embankment to gaze at the surface of the lake and say, Isn't it a fine view, my boy? and in my childish way I'd

*Lake Ogura, about ten miles in circumference, was at the southern edge of Kyoto. It was drained between 1933 and 1939.

think, Yes, it is a fine view, and admire it as I followed him. Presently we passed in front of a mansion that looked like a rich man's villa. The sounds of koto, samisen, and kokyū drifted toward us from deep within the trees.* Father stood listening at the gate for a while and then followed the wall around the broad enclosure. The tones of the koto and samisen grew clearer as I walked behind him, and I could hear faint voices, so that I knew we were approaching the inner garden. By now the wall had given way to a hedge, and Father peered into the enclosure through a spot where the foliage was thin. For some reason he stayed in that position without moving, and so I, too, pressed my face between the leaves and looked inside. There was a splendid garden with a lawn, an artificial hill, and a pond, and a room with a high floor and a balustrade had been built out over the water, in the style of the spring pavilions of ancient times. Five or six men and women were having a banquet there. It appeared to be a moon-viewing party, because a table near the end of the balustrade held offerings of food and saké, sacred lamps, and an arrangement of plumed grass and bush clover. A woman seated at the place of honor was playing the koto, and the samisen was being played by a maidservant who wore her hair in the Shimada style and was dressed like a chambermaid of old.† A man who looked like a master of the highest rank, or perhaps a teacher of polite accomplishments, was playing the kokyū. From our vantage point we couldn't see these people

---

*The kokyū is a Chinese fiddle resembling a samisen but played with a bow.
†The Shimada style was common among unmarried women and geisha.

clearly, but facing us was a golden folding screen, and before it a young maidservant, also in a Shimada, was waving a fan as she danced. I could see her movements clearly, though I couldn't make out her features. Perhaps electricity hadn't come this far yet, or perhaps these people were striving for a more tasteful atmosphere—the room was lit by candles, and the wavering flames cast their reflections on the polished columns and balustrades and on the golden screen. The moon shone brightly on the surface of the pond, and a boat was tied up at the edge: the water was drawn from Lake Ogura, and one could no doubt reach the lake directly from here by boat. Soon the dance ended, and the chambermaids took around bottles of saké. From what we could see of their respectful behavior, the woman playing the koto was their mistress and the others were serving as her companions. The time was forty years ago, when wealthy families in Kyoto and Osaka had their ladies' maids dress like servants of the shogun's daughter and taught them the proper etiquette, and if the master was a real connoisseur he would also have them learn the polite accomplishments. The villa would have belonged to a rich man of that type, and the woman playing the koto would be the young lady of the house. But she was sitting in the deepest recesses of the room and, as ill luck would have it, her face was hidden behind the arrangement of plumed grass and bush clover, so that we couldn't see what she looked like. Father tried other positions up and down along the hedge, apparently determined to have a better look, but the flower arrangement was always in the way. Her hairstyle, her makeup, and the shade of her kimono suggested that she was still young. Her voice was particularly youthful. She was too far away for us to follow her conversation, but her voice carried beyond all the others as occasional phrases in Osaka style—*"sō kai naa"* or *"sō dessharo naa"*—echoed toward us across the garden. It was a resonant voice, graceful, vivacious, and expressive. Apparently she was a little intoxicated—she laughed brightly from time to time, and her laughter sounded gay, refined, and guileless at the same time. "Father, those people are having a moon-viewing party, aren't they?" I asked. "Yes, so it seems," said Father, not moving his face from the hedge. "But whose house is this? Do you know, Father?" This time he only grunted as he peered eagerly through the hedge, his attention focused entirely on the party. We were there a long time; it seems so even in retrospect. While we watched, the maids rose two or three times to trim the candles, there was another dance, and we heard the lady sing a solo in her lovely voice as she played the koto. We watched until the party finally ended and everyone left the room, and then I was led trudging back along the top of the embankment. When I tell the story this way it must seem that I have extraordinarily vivid memories of something that happened when I was a small child, but in fact, as I mentioned a moment ago, all of this took place more than once. The next year, too, and the year after that on the Fifteenth Night, I was taken along that embankment, and when we stopped at the gate of the mansion by the lake we would hear the koto and samisen. Then Father and I would follow the wall to the hedge and peer into the garden. The room was much the same every year, with the lady and her assembled performers and chambermaids enjoying a moon-viewing banquet. What I saw the first year has become confused with what I saw in following years, but every year it was more or less as I have told you. Indeed,

I said, having been drawn into the world of reminiscences that the man narrated. And what was that mansion? Your father must have had a reason for going there every year. A reason? said the man, after some hesitation. I don't mind telling you the reason, but I fear it would be an imposition to keep you here much longer when I scarcely know you. I'd regret not hearing the rest, having heard this much; you needn't be so diffident. Thank you. If you're sure it's all right, then, I'll tell you. He took out the gourd again. Speaking of regrets, we have this much saké left. Let's finish it before I go on. He handed me the cup, and once again the saké made its pleasing gurgle as it came from the gourd.

The man continued his story after we had drained the last drop of saké: Father talked about it every year on the Fifteenth Night as we walked along the embankment. This isn't the sort of thing a child will understand, he'd say, but soon you, too, will be an adult. Remember what I've told you and try to call it to mind when you get older. I'll speak to you as if an adult were listening, and not a child. Father's face was grave whenever he said this, and he spoke as though he were with a friend his own age. At such times Father referred to the mistress of the villa as "the lady" or as "Lady Oyū." Don't forget Lady Oyū, he'd say tearfully. I bring you here every year because I want you to remember what she's like. At that age I couldn't grasp what Father said, but a child's curiosity is strong, and Father's earnestness inspired me to listen with all my might, with the result that his mood communicated itself to me and I felt that I vaguely understood. The woman he called Lady Oyū was the daughter of an Osaka family named Kosobe. She was sixteen when she married into the Kayukawa family. They chose her for her beauty, but four or five years later her husband died, and she became a widow at the age of twenty-one or twenty-two. Of course nowadays she wouldn't have to remain a widow all her life, nor would society abandon her, but this occurred early in the Meiji period, when customs from the age of the shoguns were still observed.* What's more, I'm told that the elders of her family and of the Kayukawa family were strict and, most important, that she had a son by her late husband. And so it seems that she wasn't permitted to remarry. I've also heard that Miss Oyū was cherished by her mother-in-law and husband, since she'd been carefully chosen as a bride, and was still more self-indulgent and carefree than she had been when she lived with her own family. Even after she became a widow she'd go on pleasure outings with a number of maids. Because she was free to indulge in extravagances of this sort, she appeared to an outsider to be living an easy life indeed, and it's probably true that she felt no particular discontent, enjoying as she did this continuous daily round of gaiety and diversions. When my father saw Miss Oyū for the first time she was already a widow in the circumstances I've described. I understand that he was twenty-seven—it was before I was born—and still unmarried, and Miss Oyū was twenty-two. Early in the summer, I'm told, Father had gone to the theater in Dōtombori with his younger sister and her husband—my aunt and uncle—and Miss Oyū was in the box right behind him. Miss Oyū was with a young lady of fifteen or sixteen and was attended by two young maids and an older woman who might have been her nursemaid or the head maidservant.

*The Meiji period began with the Restoration of 1868.

These three took turns fanning Miss Oyū from behind with folding fans. Seeing my aunt greet Miss Oyū, Father asked who she was. The Widow Kayukawa, came the story, and the young lady with her was her younger sister, Miss Kosobe. I was attracted to her from the first time I glimpsed her that day, Father often said. Both men and women married early then, but Father, though he was the eldest child, still remained single at twenty-seven because he'd fastidiously rejected all the marriage offers that came raining down on him. I've heard that Father frequented the teahouses and did have a favorite woman in that quarter, but when it came to marriage he didn't want such a woman for his wife. Father's tastes might be described as lordly or courtly. That is, he didn't want a chic woman but someone refined, like a lady of the court, one worthy to be dressed in a long formal robe, seated behind a curtain stand, and given the *Genji* to read; and so he wasn't going to be satisfied with a geisha. You may wonder where Father, a member of the merchant class, acquired such aristocratic tastes. Probably the explanation is that even in Osaka, families in districts like Semba were particular about their servants' manners and insisted on various formalities, more in the fashion of court aristocrats than of minor provincial lords, and Father was reared in such a household. When Father saw Miss Oyū, in any case, he sensed that she was the type he'd been thinking of so long. I don't know how he sensed this. I'm told that she was seated directly behind him; perhaps in the way she spoke to her maids, in her attitude and manner, he saw the kind of magnanimity one expects from the young lady of a great house. In her photographs Miss Oyū has full cheeks and a round, childlike face. In Father's words, There are other women with features as beautiful as hers, but there's something indistinct about her face. Her features—the eyes, the nose, the mouth—are blurred as though they were veiled by a layer of silk gauze, leaving no strong, clear lines; and when I gaze at her face a misty shadow seems to fall before my eyes, as if a haze floated about her and nowhere else. The word *rōtaketa*, used in old texts, describes such a face, and therein lies Lady Oyū's nobility, he said. Indeed, she does have that look, when one thinks of it that way. People with childlike faces generally don't lose their youthfulness unless they've been worn down by domestic problems. Miss Oyū has always had the fresh face of a girl, my aunt often said; her features have been the same, from the time she was fifteen or sixteen up into her mid-forties. And so Father was drawn at once by Miss Oyū's indistinct *rōtaketa* quality, and when I look at Miss Oyū's photograph with Father's tastes in mind, I can see why he would have liked her. In short, she has a quality about her that recalls the subtle ladies of the court, a classical aroma in the midst of radiant good cheer, such as one senses in the face of an old Izukura doll. Such an aroma hovers somewhere in Miss Oyū's face. My aunt, Father's younger sister of whom I spoke before, had been a childhood friend of Miss Oyū's and as a girl studied with the same koto master, and so she knew all about Miss Oyū's upbringing, family, and marriage. She told Father what she knew: though Miss Oyū had several sisters—one older and one younger, in addition to the younger sister Miss Oyū had taken to the theater—she received special treatment as her parents' favorite, and all her whims were indulged. One reason may have been that Miss Oyū was the most beautiful of the sisters, but my aunt says that the sisters themselves seemed to think of her as someone special and to take it for granted that everyone else would think so too. Being "a person of character," to borrow my aunt's words, Miss Oyū didn't ask people to treat her this way, nor was she arrogant or pushy, but everyone was extremely kind to her, waiting on her as if she were a princess and allowing her to do as she pleased, determined not to let her suffer the slightest anxiety. They sought to keep her untouched by the everyday troubles of the world, even if it meant sacrificing themselves for her sake. It was Miss Oyū's nature to make everyone who came near her feel this way, including her parents, sisters, and friends. When my aunt visited Miss Oyū as a girl, Miss Oyū was treated as though she were the Kosobe family treasure. She never did the smallest chore herself, and her sisters looked after her like chambermaids; nor was there anything unnatural about this, my aunt said—Miss Oyū seemed to accept the attention with the greatest innocence. Hearing this account from my aunt, Father liked Miss Oyū all the more, but he had no opportunity to see her until my aunt learned that Miss Oyū was to be in a koto recital and said to Father, I'll go with you if you want to see Miss Oyū. On the day of the recital, Miss Oyū wore her hair hanging straight down in back, put on a long formal robe, and had incense burning as she played *Yuya*.* Yes, even today it's customary to observe formalities like these when one plays a composition that's licensed by a master. People spend great sums of money for the purpose. The masters are eager to have their wealthy pupils perform, and Miss Oyū, taking koto lessons to relieve her boredom, had probably been encouraged by her master. As

*A composition by Yamada Kengyō (1757–1817), based on the nō play of the same name by Zeami (1363–1443).

I said before, I've heard Miss Oyū sing and know the beauty of her voice, and now when I consider her personality and recall that voice, I sense her refinement all the more keenly. Father was extremely moved the day he heard Miss Oyū sing for the first time. The sight of Miss Oyū wearing a long formal robe, which he'd never expected to see, made a reality of the vision he'd adored in his dreams. He must have been so surprised and delighted that he doubted his eyes. Apparently Miss Oyū was still wearing the formal robe when my aunt went to the dressing room after the performance. The koto was of no importance, she said, but I did want a chance to dress like this just once. Reluctant to take off the robe, she added, And now I'm going to have my picture taken. When he heard about this, Father realized that Miss Oyū's tastes matched his own. He decided he could take no one but Miss Oyū for his wife. He sensed that the person he'd waited for so long, sketching her image in his heart, was none other than Miss Oyū. When he confided this to my aunt, she sympathized with his feelings, but knowing the situation, she told him marriage with Miss Oyū would be impossible. Something might be arranged were it not for the child, she said, but Miss Oyū had a baby to rear, the precious son and heir of the family. She was in no position to abandon him and leave the Kayukawas. Moreover, Miss Oyū had a mother-in-law, and her father was in good health, though her mother was dead. These family elders had been moved by affection to let Miss Oyū have her way, because they sympathized with her position as a young widow and wanted to help her forget her loneliness. Implied in this was their wish that, in exchange, she remain faithful to her husband for the rest of her life. Miss Oyū understood, my aunt said. Despite her luxurious way of life, there had never been any rumors of misconduct. It was clear that the lady herself had no intention of marrying again, she said. Still unwilling to give up, Father said in that case he wouldn't speak of marriage, but would my aunt act as intermediary and arrange for them to meet from time to time? He'd be satisfied just to see her face. My aunt found it difficult to refuse Father again when he was so persistent, but his request was difficult because she and Miss Oyū had been only girls when they were intimate, and by now they'd grown apart. Thinking it over, she finally proposed that Father marry Miss Oyū's younger sister instead; since he had no wish to marry anyone but Miss Oyū, he should settle for the sister, there was no hope of a marriage with Miss Oyū herself, but the prospects with her younger sister would be excellent. The younger sister she spoke of was Oshizu, the girl Miss Oyū had taken to the theater. The sister between Miss Oyū and Miss Oshizu was already spoken for, and Miss Oshizu had reached the perfect age. Father remembered her face, having seen her at the theater, and he seems to have given my aunt's suggestion a great deal of thought: Miss Oshizu was not unattractive herself, and though her features were different from Miss Oyū's, the women were sisters nonetheless and there was something about Miss Oshizu that recalled Miss Oyū; the main objection was that Miss Oshizu lacked the *rōtaketa* quality of Miss Oyū's face; she seemed to rank far below Miss Oyū; it was not so noticeable when he looked at Miss Oshizu by herself, but when she was with Miss Oyū the difference was as great as that between a princess and a chambermaid; for that reason he might never have considered Miss Oshizu if she hadn't been Miss Oyū's sister, but since she was her sister, and the same blood flowed in her body, he liked Miss Oshizu too. This didn't mean that it was easy for him to make up his mind and settle for Miss Oshizu. First of all, it would be unfair to Miss Oshizu to marry her with such a motive; further, he was determined forever to cling to his pure admiration for Miss Oyū, to keep her always as his secret, spiritual wife; he could never be content with a different wife, even if she was Miss Oyū's younger sister. On the other hand, if he took the younger sister as his bride, he'd be able to meet Miss Oyū frequently and speak with her, but if he did not, he'd never see her face again except when he was blessed by chance. This thought made him feel unbearably lonely. After vacillating for a long time, Father finally agreed to have a formal meeting with Miss Oshizu as his prospective bride. To tell the truth, he still had no desire to marry her—actually he wanted to see Miss Oyū again, if only once, using the meeting as a pretext. In this he succeeded, for Miss Oyū came to all the meetings and preliminary discussions. There was no mother in the Kosobe house to accompany Miss Oshizu, and what is more, Miss Oshizu was spending half of every month with the Kayukawas, since Miss Oyū had nothing but time on her hands, so that it was hard to know whose daughter Miss Oshizu was. It was natural, then, for Miss Oyū to make frequent appearances, and Father could hardly have asked for anything better. Since seeing her was his main objective, he dragged out the discussions as long as he could, holding two or three formal meetings and delaying for about six months, with the result that Miss Oyū began to call frequently at my aunt's house. During that time she also had occasion to speak with Father and gradually came to know him. One day she asked him, Do you dislike Oshizu? When Father replied that he did not dislike her, she said, Then please accept her as your bride, and eagerly promoted the match. Apparently she was even more direct with my aunt, saying that of all her sisters she was closest to this one and wanted to see her marry a man like Mr. Seribashi; she would be happy to have such a man for her younger brother. It was entirely because of what Miss Oyū said that Father finally made up his mind, and before long Oshizu was married. Yes, this means that Oshizu is my mother and Miss Oyū my aunt; but it's not that simple. I don't know how Father took Miss Oyū's words, but on her wedding night Oshizu said, I've come as your bride because I know my sister's heart. I couldn't face her if I gave myself to you. Make her happy, I beg you—I don't mind being your wife in name only. And with this she began to cry.

Father thought he was dreaming when he heard Oshizu's words. Though he was secretly in love with Miss Oyū, he had had no idea that she appreciated his devotion, and it certainly had never occurred to him that she might love him. How do you know what your sister is feeling? he pressed the weeping Oshizu. You must have some evidence for saying this. Has your sister confided in you? She wouldn't tell me such a thing, nor would I ask her, but I understand nonetheless, Oshizu said. It may seem strange that Oshizu—my mother—had sensed all this when she was still an unsophisticated girl, but something I learned later explains it. At first the Kosobes had decided to decline Father's proposal, saying that the age difference was too great, and Miss Oyū was ready to go along with them; but one day when Oshizu went to visit her, Miss Oyū said, I think it's a splendid match, but I can't very well push it when the others feel as they do—after all, he's not going to be *my* son-in-law. If you don't dislike him, Shizu, how would it be if *you* asked them to keep the negotiations alive? Then I'll step in and arrange everything for you. Oshizu had no definite thoughts on the matter. He couldn't be a bad man if you like him so much, she said. If you think it's right, then I'll do as you say. I'm happy to hear you say so, said Miss Oyū. A difference of eleven or twelve years isn't unheard of. Most important, I have a feeling that he and I will get along. Sisters become strangers to each other when they marry, and I'd rather you weren't taken away by anyone, but in this case I won't feel you've been taken away; it'll be more like gaining a brother. I know it sounds as though I'm pushing him on you for my own purposes, but if he's good for me, then he's certain to be good for you as well. Think of it as devotion to your big sister, and do as I say about this. If you were to marry someone I disliked, I'd have no one to keep me company and I'd be so lonely I couldn't bear it, she concluded. As I said before, Miss Oyū was treated with affection by everyone and was unaware of her own self-centeredness because of the way she'd been brought up; probably she was just presuming on her favorite sister's love. But Oshizu thought she detected something else in Miss Oyū's manner. The more self-centered and unreasonable her words, the more lovable Miss Oyū appeared, and this time perhaps there was a kind of passion in her innocence. Even if Miss Oyū didn't intend it, Oshizu must have sensed it. Oshizu probably caught other signs as well: bashful women like her tend to be observant despite their reticence. For that matter, they say that Miss Oyū's color suddenly improved after she came to know Father and that she seemed to enjoy nothing more than to talk with Oshizu about him. He said to Oshizu, You're letting your imagination run away with you. Afraid that she'd notice how his heart was pounding, he pretended to be hurt: We've become man and wife because of a bond from a former life; won't you look upon our marriage as something that was fated, even if it seems to be lacking in some respects? Your devotion to your older sister is a fine thing, I'm sure, but it would go against her own wishes for you to jump to conclusions and maintain this illogical loyalty to her while you treat me heartlessly. Surely she doesn't wish for anything of the sort, and she'd be distressed if she heard about it, he said.

But you married me because you wanted to be my sister's brother, didn't you? She heard as much from your sister, and so I knew about it too. Isn't it true that you've received a great many good offers of marriage, but none of them pleased you? It's only because of my sister that such an exacting man would marry a stupid thing like me, she said. Father hung his head, at a loss how to reply. My sister would be overjoyed if I told her just a word of what you truly feel, but that would only lead to reserve on both sides, and so I'll say nothing to her now; but please, hide nothing from me, or I'll think ill of you, she said. I understand. I didn't know you'd married me out of such thoughtfulness. I'll never forget your kindness, said Father. Weeping, he continued, Still, I only think of her as a sister, and whatever you may do for us, I can't think of her any other way. She and I will only suffer if you maintain this rash loyalty to her. It can't be pleasant for you, but if you don't hate me, won't you think of it as devotion to your sister to be my wife and stop being so distant? And let's both honor her as our elder sister, he said. How could I be so wicked as to hate you or find anything unpleasant? I've always followed my sister in everything; if she is fond of you, then so am I. Properly speaking, I shouldn't have come to you, because it's wrong for me to take the man my sister loves; and yet I thought that if I didn't come, decorum would prevent you two from continuing your relationship, and so I've married you in the hope that you'll accept me as your younger sister. Father said, Then do you intend to bury yourself like a piece of bogwood for your sister's sake? I doubt that she's the kind of woman who'd be content to let her sister do such a thing. Aren't you maligning a pure, innocent person? She replied, It distresses me for you to take it that way. Of course I want to protect my sister's purity. If she's going to remain faithful to my late brother-in-law, then I'll remain chaste for her sake. I won't be the only one to bury herself. Isn't my sister doing the same thing? Perhaps you don't know that my sister was born with a disposition and a beauty that make people love her, and the entire household strives with one mind to protect her as though they'd been entrusted with the child of a daimyo; but now that she's met you she's bound by loathsome rules. I'd surely be cursed if I stole you away from her, knowing this. If she heard, she'd say, Don't be ridiculous, and so I hope you'll keep it to yourself. It doesn't matter whether anyone else knows about it; I'll do what I must to satisfy myself. If someone born to happiness and good fortune like my sister can't have her way in this world, then I amount to nothing at all. From the start I decided to come as your bride with the intention of making my sister happier. I beg you to make the same resolve and remain faithful to her, though in front of others we behave as though we were man and wife. If you can't muster the strength to bear this, then you don't love my sister half as much as I do. Hearing this,

Father became obsessed with the thought that if Oshizu was prepared to sacrifice herself to this degree, then as a man he could hardly do less. Thank you, he said. I admire you for saying what you've said. My true wish has always been to live as a widower as long as your sister remains a widow. I've spoken as I have only because I thought it would be cruel to let you live like a nun, but now that I've heard of your saintly intentions I can't find the words to express my gratitude. With you so determined, what objection could I have? It may seem heartless, but the truth is that I, too, prefer it this way. I should have been the one to make the request of you, but I wasn't in a position to do so. I'll say nothing more and accept your great kindness. With this he lifted Oshizu's hands reverently to his forehead. They talked through the night without sleeping a wink.

To society, then, Father and Oshizu looked like an affectionate couple who had never once quarreled, but in fact they didn't sleep together as man and wife, and Miss Oyū didn't know about their pledge to be loyal to her. Seeing how well they got along together, Miss Oyū was very pleased with herself. What a good thing we did as I said, she boasted to her family. She and the couple visited each other almost every day thereafter, and the Seribashis always accompanied her to the theater and on her outings. I hear that they often invited each other for one- or two-night trips. On these occasions Miss Oyū and the couple would sleep side by side in the same room. Gradually this became their habit, so that even when they weren't on a trip Miss Oyū would invite the couple to stay with her, or be invited to stay with them. Long afterward Father told me nostalgically that when it was time to retire, Miss Oyū would say, Warm my feet, Shizu, and pull Oshizu into bed with her. Warming Miss Oyū's feet was Oshizu's role because her body was especially warm, whereas Miss Oyū's feet were so cold she couldn't sleep. Miss Oyū said, I've had a maid to take your place since you married, Shizu, but it just doesn't go as well as when you do it; and since I'm accustomed to you, foot-warmers and hot-water bottles just aren't enough. You needn't hesitate to ask, Oshizu would reply, climbing happily into bed with her. I came to stay with you so I could help you as before; and she'd lie beside Miss Oyū until her sister went to sleep or said, All right. I've heard many other stories about Miss Oyū's pampered life. She had three or four maids to take care of her at home. When she washed her hands, one maid would ladle the water while another stood by with a towel, and the moment Miss Oyū held out her dripping hands the maid with the towel would carefully dry them. Thus she hardly ever used her own hands, whether it was to put on a stocking or to wash herself in the bath. Yes, that might seem extravagant for someone born into the merchant class, even in those days, but when she married into the Kayukawa family her father made it a point to say, I brought my daughter up this way, and we can't very well ask her to change her habits now. If you are truly devoted to her, won't you let her go on as she is accustomed? And so, they say, she kept the generous disposition of her childhood, even after she was married and had a child. Visiting Miss Oyū was like calling on a court lady in her chambers, Father often said. It probably struck him this way because of his own tastes, but he said the furnishings in Miss Oyū's room were all in the palace style or decorated with designs favored by the aristocracy, and everything from the towel rack to the chamber pot was waxed and lacquered. Instead of a single-panel screen at the door between the anteroom and her room, she had a clothes rack draped with a different robe every day. And while there was no dais in her inner room, Miss Oyū did sit leaning on an armrest. When she had nothing else to do she'd scent a robe with aloes, compare different incenses with her chambermaids, play the fan-throwing game, or sit at the go board. Since she insisted on elegance even in her games but wasn't very good at go, she'd play five-in-a-row just so she could make use of her favorite board, a fifteenth-century lacquer piece with an autumn-flower design. For all three meals she'd sit at a tray that might have come from a doll set, and eat from lacquered bowls. When she was thirsty a handmaid would approach respectfully with a tea-bowl stand, and when she wanted to smoke, a maid would sit beside her to fill the long pipe and light it. At night she slept behind a low folding screen decorated in the Kōrin style;* when she awakened on cold mornings she'd have oiled paper spread on the floor and wash her face right there, with a pitcher and a basin, as the maids carried hot and cold water to her. Since she was this way in everything, outings were complicated affairs. At least one maid would always accompany her when she went on a trip; Oshizu would look after one thing and another, and even Father would help. Carrying Miss Oyū's luggage, dressing her, massaging her—each one would assume a role to ensure that Miss Oyū wanted for nothing. Yes, her child had been weaned by then, and an old woman looked after him. Miss Oyū hardly ever took him along. But one evening when they'd gone to Yoshino

*Named for Ogata Kōrin (1658–1716), a painter noted for his bold composition and rich colors.

for blossom-viewing, Miss Oyū complained that her
breasts were swollen and asked Oshizu to suck at them as
soon as they arrived at the inn. Watching them, Father said,
You're very good at it, and laughed. I'm used to drinking
her milk, Oshizu said. She's had me do it now and then ever
since Hajime was born, because the child gets his milk from
his nurse. What does it taste like? he asked. I don't remember how it tasted when I was a baby, but now it has an oddly
sweet taste. Why don't you try some too? she said. With a
teacup she caught some of the drops that fell from the
nipple and offered the cup to Father. He took a sip. Yes, it
is sweet, he said, pretending to be casual about it. Oshizu
must have offered the milk to him for a reason, he thought;
he blushed and felt like running away. My mouth feels
funny, he said, and Miss Oyū laughed gaily when he
stepped out onto the veranda. Oshizu began to play all
kinds of pranks on Father after that; perhaps she enjoyed
seeing him embarrassed or flustered. People were likely to
be around them during the day, but on the rare occasions
when the three were alone together, Oshizu would
abruptly get up and leave the other two by themselves for
a long time, and then she'd suddenly reappear just as Father began to get nervous. When they sat in a row, she'd
always have Father sit next to Miss Oyū. When they
played cards or other games, she'd make sure that Father
sat opposite Miss Oyū as her opponent. When Miss Oyū
asked for help with her sash, Oshizu would have Father do
it, claiming that it required a man's strength; when they
helped Miss Oyū put on new footwear, Oshizu would say
the clasps were tight and get Father to help; and she'd
watch Father's embarrassment and bewilderment every
time. To all appearances this was innocent mischief; Father

knew there was no spite or malice in it. Oshizu may have been acting out of kindness—perhaps she thought that behaving this way would break down the reserve between Father and Miss Oyū, and that the momentum of events would lead them presently to open their hearts to each other. She seemed to be praying that momentum would build, that the two of them would commit some awkward blunder.

But life went on uneventfully for the two of them, until one day there was an incident between Oshizu and Miss Oyū. Knowing nothing about it, Father went to visit Miss Oyū; and the moment she saw him she turned away to hide her tears. Nothing of the sort had ever happened before. Is something wrong? he asked Oshizu. She knows, Oshizu said. It came to a point where I had to say something, and I told her. But Oshizu said nothing more—she didn't describe the events that led up to this development, and so Father couldn't quite understand what she'd done. Probably Oshizu saw that the time had come to confess the truth—her sister would be embarrassed and would give them a lecture when she learned that they weren't really husband and wife, but after all this time she'd be swayed by her affection for them. Oshizu would have watched her sister closely and chosen the right moment to bring the conversation around to this topic. She had a way of reading people carefully and moving things along, and perhaps because she took things a little too seriously, something about her reminded one of an elderly geisha clever at arranging liaisons. Now that I think about it, she seemed to have been born to dedicate herself body and soul to Miss Oyū. Nothing in the world makes me happier than being able to help my sister, she said; I don't know why I feel that

way, but when I see her face I forget all about myself. It's
true that Oshizu might be called meddlesome, but Miss
Oyū and Father both realized that it sprang from her selfless love for her sister, and they could only weep tears of
gratitude. At first Miss Oyū was astonished. I had no idea
I'd brought about such a crime. It makes me fear for the
next life, she said with a shudder. But they could cancel
their pact, she added, and begged them to live like a real
couple. It's not as if we're doing this at your request, Oshizu
replied. Both Shinnosuke and I are doing what we want to
do. There's no reason for you to worry, whatever may
happen. It was wrong of me to say anything. It'd be best if
you pretended you hadn't heard anything. Since they
wouldn't listen to her, Miss Oyū refrained from visiting the
couple for a while, but she couldn't do anything that might
give offense, because all the relatives knew how close they
were. Presently the two sides drew together again, and
Oshizu's plan went smoothly in the end. Yes, if we could
see into Miss Oyū's heart, we might find that something in
her had relaxed, as though the restraints she'd woven about
herself had been loosened. She probably couldn't bring
herself to resent her sister's fidelity. Thereafter Miss Oyū's
innate magnanimity showed itself again and she let the
couple do as they wished. She trusted in their discretion,
and whether she recognized their solicitude or not, she
grew to accept it unquestioningly. It was around this time
that Father began to refer to Miss Oyū as Lady Oyū. Once
when he and Oshizu were talking about her, Oshizu told
him to stop referring to her as their older sister, and so he
called her Lady Oyū, thinking this name fit her best. Soon
he was using it all the time, and when it slipped out in Miss
Oyū's presence, she said she liked it and hoped that he'd

call her that when they were alone together. Then she said, I'm grateful to everyone for being so good to me, but I want you to understand that I was brought up to take such treatment for granted. I'm always in a good mood when people make a fuss over me. I'll give you a few examples of Miss Oyū's childlike willfulness. Once she held her hand in front of Father's nose and said, I want you to hold your breath until I say all right. Father made a great effort but finally let a little breath escape. I haven't said all right yet, Miss Oyū cried peevishly. So she'd close his lips with her fingers or use a folded piece of red Shioze crepe to cover his mouth. At times like this, Father said, her face would look like the face of a kindergarten child, and one could hardly believe that she was a woman over twenty. Another time she said, Don't look at my face that way; put your hands together and sit formally, with your eyes down. She'd tell him not to laugh as she tickled him under the chin and in the ribs; or she'd say, I forbid you to say ouch, and pinch him all over. She was extremely fond of this kind of mischief. You mustn't go to sleep, she'd say, even if I do. If you get sleepy, fight it off and stare at my face as I sleep. She'd doze off peacefully, and Father would begin to feel drowsy and dreamy too; but then she'd be awake and blowing into his ear or tickling his face with a piece of twisted paper to make him wake up. Father said that Miss Oyū was born with a sense of theater; her thoughts and gestures were spontaneously theatrical, which enhanced her cheerful personality and added to her charm without ever seeming artificial or affected; and the greatest difference between Oshizu and Miss Oyū was that Oshizu lacked this sense of theater. No one but Miss Oyū could have been in her element playing the koto in a long formal robe, or sitting behind a curtain of robes and drinking saké from a lacquered cup as a chambermaid poured for her.

Of course it was because of Oshizu's efforts on their behalf that their relationship could develop this way, and because Miss Oyū spent so much time at the Seribashi house, there being fewer people around than in the Kayukawa household. Oshizu used her wits in many ways. Don't you think it's a waste of money to take a maid along on a trip? she'd say. You won't want for anything if I'm with you. This made it possible for the three of them to go alone to the shrines at Ise and Kotohira. Dressing plainly like a maid, Oshizu would have her bedding laid out in the anteroom. The three of them would adjust their relationships to the occasion and take care how they addressed one another. When they stayed at an inn, it might have been simplest for Miss Oyū and Father just to act as man and wife, but since Miss Oyū tended to assume the role of mistress, Father would pretend to be her butler or steward or pose as an artist under her patronage. He and Oshizu would call her Madam when they traveled. This was one of Miss Oyū's favorite games. She didn't drink much, but she'd grow quite bold when she'd had a little saké at dinnertime and burst into gay laughter even when she had seemed to be calm and relaxed. But here I must say something in defense of both Miss Oyū and Father—though their relationship had advanced this far, neither of them allowed it to go all the way. Oh, I suppose one could say that by now it made little difference whether they did or not, and it's no defense just to say that they didn't; but I want to believe Father. To Oshizu he said, After all that has happened, it's not a question of doing wrong by you, but I swear by the gods and Buddhas that we are faithful to you even when we sleep side by side. This may not be what you want, but Lady Oyū and I both would fear for our souls if we humiliated you that much. And so, well, we refrain for our own peace of mind. Probably it was as he said, but it would seem that another factor was their concern for what would happen if Miss Oyū conceived. Still, chastity can be interpreted broadly or narrowly; perhaps I can't say that Miss Oyū was unblemished. In this connection I remember that Father cherished a set of Miss Oyū's winter robes, which he kept in a paulownia box that bore the inscription Aloeswood Incense in Miss Oyū's calligraphy. Once, he showed me the contents of the box. Pulling out a long Yūzen underrobe from the bottom, he held it out to me and said, Miss Oyū wore this against her skin. See how heavy the crepe is. I took it in my hands. It was quite unlike the modern fabric—the crepe of those days was deeply crimped and the threads were thick, so that it seemed as heavy as chain mail. Heavy, don't you think? he asked. It truly is, I said. He nodded as though my answer gratified him. Crepe doesn't have to be limp and soft, he said; the real value of the material is in this heavy crimping. You can feel the softness of a woman's skin all the better if you touch her body through these heavy crimps. Crepe looks rougher and more beautiful and feels better to the touch, the smoother the skin of the person wearing it. Miss Oyū was born with delicate hands and feet, and their delicacy showed all the more clearly when she wore this heavy crepe. He held up the robe with both hands. I don't know how her body supported this much weight, he said with a sigh. He rubbed his cheek against it as though he were embracing her.

Then you must have been quite grown up by the time

your father showed you the underrobe, I said, having listened to the man's story in silence up to this point. I should
think it would be difficult for a young boy to understand
something like that. No, I was still only about ten, but
Father spoke as though I were an adult. I didn't understand
at the time, of course, but I remembered his words and
gradually worked out their meaning as I matured. I see.
Then let me ask you this: If the relationship between Miss
Oyū and your father was as you say, then whose child are
you? You may well ask. I can't bring my story to a close
without telling you that, and so I beg you to listen just a
little longer. The curious love between Father and Miss
Oyū that I've described went on for only a short time—just
three or four years, beginning when Miss Oyū was twenty-
three or -four. Then, when Miss Oyū was in her twenty-
seventh year, I believe it was, Hajime, her child by her late
husband, died of pneumonia after a case of the measles.
The child's death affected Miss Oyū's circumstances and,
in turn, Father's whole life. For some time before that, Miss
Oyū's all-too-frequent visits with her sister and brother-in-
law had gradually become a subject of comment—not
among the Kosobes, who said nothing about it, but among
her mother-in-law and other relatives in the Kayukawa
family, and there were those who said they couldn't imagine what Oshizu had in mind. However skillfully Oshizu
may have played her part, it was natural that people would
start to regard her with suspicion in the long run. Seribashi's bride is too good to be true, they'd say, and sisterly
devotion has its limits. As the backbiting became more of
a problem, my aunt, who had guessed the truth, was the
only person who worried about the three of them. The
Kayukawa family had paid no attention to the gossip at

first, but when Hajime died, even they criticized Miss Oyū
for having been inattentive to him. There's no denying that
Miss Oyū was at fault in this. I doubt that her love for the
child had diminished, but she had long been in the habit of
leaving him in an old woman's care. They say she slipped
away from the sickbed for half a day, and it was in that
interval that the child suddenly developed pneumonia.
Miss Oyū was important to the family while the child lived,
but after his death—well, recently there'd been unflatter-
ing rumors, and she was still very young; it might be best
to send her back to her own family before things get complicated, they said. Would her family take her back? After
complex negotiations over this and other matters, the families agreed on conditions for Miss Oyū's amicable removal
from the Kayukawa family register, in such a way that no
one was hurt. And so Miss Oyū returned to the Kosobe
family. Her elder brother, who had succeeded as head of
the family, didn't treat her unkindly—she had, after all,
been her parents' favorite, and he resented the way the
Kayukawa family had treated her; but things weren't the
same as when her parents were still living, and she must
have sensed a certain reserve. Oshizu urged her to come to
her house if she felt constrained at the Kosobes', but her
brother forbade it, saying they should be discreet as long as
people were spreading rumors about them. In Oshizu's
view, her brother may have known the truth, and one
reason for thinking so is that about one year later he urged
Miss Oyū to remarry. The man was a saké maker from
Fushimi named Miyazu. Though he was much older than
Miss Oyū, he often visited the Kayukawas and had been
familiar with her spirited nature for a long time. He was
eager for the match, his wife having died recently. He made

a splendid proposal, I'm told: If Miss Oyū agreed to marry him, he wouldn't leave her in the shop at Fushimi; he'd enlarge his villa on Lake Ogura, adding a wing in the tea-cottage style she preferred, and have her live there. He'd treat her with the utmost respect and see that she lived in greater luxury even than when she lived with the Kayukawas. Her brother was enthusiastic and urged Miss Oyū to accept. Good fortune follows you around, he said. Why don't you marry him and put those gossipmongers to shame? What's more, he summoned Father and Oshizu and pressed them to broach the subject delicately with her and convince her to accept, so as to give the lie to the rumors. If Father had been determined to carry his love through to the end, he would have had no choice at this point but to commit suicide with Miss Oyū. In fact, I'm told that he came to this resolve more than a few times, but Oshizu's presence made it impossible for him to follow through. In short, Father thought it would be wrong to leave Oshizu behind, but he didn't want her to die with him and Miss Oyū. Oshizu, too, was afraid she'd be left behind. Take me with you, she begged, I couldn't bear to be left out after all this. I'm told that this was the only time she ever sounded jealous. Another factor, which weakened Father's resolve even more, was his compassion for Miss Oyū. It was most fitting for a person like her to go on forever fresh and innocent, served by a crowd of chambermaids and living in splendor; and to let such a person die would be heartbreaking. This thought influenced him more than anything else, he said. He confided his feelings to Miss Oyū. You are far too good for me to take as my companion in death. An ordinary woman might die for love, but you are blessed with an abundance of good fortune and character. To throw these qualities away would be to lose your nobility. So please go and live in that mansion at Lake Ogura, behind its gorgeous panels and screens. I'll be happier imagining you there than I would be dying with you. When I say this, I know that you won't think my heart has changed or that I'm afraid to die. It's because such petty notions would never cross your mind that I'm able to speak with confidence. You were born with the magnanimity to give up a man like me with a smile. Listening in silence to Father's words, Miss Oyū let a tear fall, but then cheerfully lifted her face. Yes, I think you're right, she said. Let's do as you say. She didn't seem at all disconcerted, nor did she offer any contrived apologies. Father said that Miss Oyū had never looked so grand and elegant as at that moment.

And so Miss Oyū was soon remarried in Fushimi; but her husband Miyazu was a playboy, I'm told, and had married her on a whim. He tired of Miss Oyū almost immediately and hardly ever went near her villa again, they say. Nevertheless, he spared no expense on her household, saying that a woman like her must be kept on display like an ornament in the alcove, so that Miss Oyū continued to live as before in a world like the *Rustic Genji* illustrations.* In Osaka, on the other hand, the Kosobe family and Father's family went into decline from that time on, and, as I said before, by the time Mother died we'd fallen to the point of living in a back-alley tenement. Yes, the Mother I'm referring to is Oshizu. I was borne by Oshizu. Considering the hardships she'd endured so long, and moved to an

---

Fake Murasaki and the Rustic Genji (1829) was written by Ryūtei Tanehiko (1783–1842) and illustrated with great charm by Utagawa Kunisada (1786–1864).

indescribable sympathy by the fact that she was Miss Oyū's younger sister, Father consummated his marriage with Oshizu after he'd parted with Miss Oyū. With this the man stopped, as though he was tired from talking so long, and pulled the smoking case from his sash.

Thank you for a most interesting story. Now I understand why your father took you as a boy to wander outside the villa at Lake Ogura. But I believe you said that you've gone there every year since to view the moon. In fact, you said you were on your way there this very night, as I remember. Yes, he replied, I'm about to set out again tonight. If I go behind the villa on the Fifteenth Night and peer through the hedge even now, Miss Oyū will be playing the koto and her chambermaids will be dancing for her. That's odd, I thought. But Miss Oyū would be nearly eighty years old by now, wouldn't she? I asked, but there was only the rustle of the wind blowing across the grasses. I could not see the reeds that covered the shore, and the man had vanished as though he had melted into the light of the moon.

Captain
Shigemoto's
Mother

Heijū. Nickname of Taira Sadafun (870?–923?). Assistant Commander in the Military Guards. A famous amorist and poet, lover of Shigemoto's mother, Jijū, and others.

Jijū of Hon'in (dates unknown). A serving woman at Shihei's Hon'in Mansion. Cruel lover of Heijū.

Shihei. Nickname of Fujiwara Tokihira (871–909), Hon'in Minister of the Left and the most powerful man of his time. Nephew of Kunitsune. Second husband of Shigemoto's mother. Putative father of Atsutada. Posthumously named Honorary Chancellor.

Sugawara Michizane (845–903). Minister of the Right. Celebrated statesman and poet. Political rival of Shihei, who banished him in 901.

Fujiwara Kunitsune (828–908). Governor-General Major Counselor. Uncle of Shihei, first husband of Shigemoto's mother, father of Shigemoto and perhaps of Atsutada.

Shigemoto's mother (884?– ?). "The Ariwara lady," granddaughter of the great poet Ariwara Narihira. Wife of Kunitsune and of Shihei; lover of Heijū; mother of Shigemoto and Atsutada. Her given name is not known.

Fujiwara Shigemoto (900?– ?). Lesser Captain of the Left Bodyguards. Son of Kunitsune, elder brother of Atsutada.

Fujiwara Atsutada (905?–943). Middle Counselor. Poet and musician. Son of Shigemoto's mother and Shihei, or perhaps Kunitsune. Shigemoto's younger brother.

flask; and when the unsuspecting Heijū moistened his eyes
with the inky water, the woman held up a mirror and
recited a poem: "That you are two-faced you have shown
me before, but how can I countenance this, your visage
stained with ink and you married to another?" *The Rivers
and Seas Commentary* cites *Tales of Times Now Past* as the
original source of this story and mentions that it also appears in *Tales of Yamato*, but it is not to be found in either
book as they survive today.* All the same, the story of
Heijū's inkstain must already have been well known in
Murasaki Shikibu's day as a tale of a bungling amorist,
since she put a joke like this in Genji's mouth.†

Many poems by Heijū are preserved in *The Ancient and
Modern Collection*‡ and other royal anthologies, his geneal-
ogy is fairly clear, and he appears in various tales of the
time, and so it is certain that he was a real person, but the
year of his death is unclear, being given as 923 or 928, and
the year of his birth is not recorded anywhere. *Tales of
Times Now Past* reports: "There was a man named Taira
Sadafun, an Assistant Commander in the Military Guards.
His nickname was Heijū. He was not lowborn, being the
grandson of a royal prince. He was the leading amorist of
the day, and there were few wives and daughters and court
ladies whom he had not made love to." Elsewhere it says:
"Heijū's breeding was good, his appearance beautiful. His
manner and address were so appealing that no one in those

Tales of Times Now Past (Konjaku monogatari): a collection of tales
probably compiled early in the twelfth century. *Tales of Yamato
(Yamato monogatari):* a tenth-century collection of poem-tales.
†*The Tale of Genji* was written by Murasaki Shikibu early in the
eleventh century.
‡*Kokinshū*, compiled ca. 905.

✿ THIS TALE BEGINS with the famous amorist Heijū.

The "Safflower" chapter in *The Tale of Genji* concludes
with this scene: "Feeling sorry for him, she drew close,
moistened a piece of Michinoku paper in the water jar by
his inkstone, and rubbed. Don't color me like Heijū, he said
playfully. Being red is enough to bear." In this passage
Genji has deliberately dabbed his nose with red watercolor
and pretended that no amount of rubbing will remove it.
Growing anxious, the eleven-year-old Murasaki moistens
a piece of paper and begins to rub Genji's nose herself,
whereupon Genji quips, "I can live with the red, but I don't
want to be daubed with black as Heijū was." According to
*The Rivers and Seas Commentary,** one of the old *Genji* com-
mentaries, Genji's joke is based on an old story: Long ago,
Heijū pretended to weep when he visited a certain woman,
but the tears would not always come when he needed them.
He took a flask of water from his writing set and slipped it
into the folds of his kimono to use for moistening his eyes.
Catching on, the woman put some freshly ground ink in the

*Kakaishō, 1367.

days surpassed him. This being the case, there was not a wife or daughter—much less court ladies—who had not received his attention." His real name, then, was Taira Sadafun; he was a grandson of Emperor Kammu's grandson Prince Mochiyo, and the son of Taira Yoshikaze, Middle Captain of the Right Bodyguards, Junior Fourth Rank, Upper Grade. There are several theories about the nickname Heijū, which means "Taira middle." According to one, the name came from his being the second of three sons. Another has it that his Chinese-style sobriquet was Chū, written with a slightly different character than that for "middle." (The syllable *chū* in his nickname should be voiced, according to *The Blossom Game Commentary.**) "Heijū" probably was coined in imitation of Ariwara Narihira's nickname, "Zaigo Chūjō," or "Ariwara Fifth-Son Middle Captain."†

Indeed, Narihira and Heijū resemble each other closely on a number of points. Both were descended from the royal family and were born in the early Heian period; both were handsome and amorous, and both were skilled poets, Narihira being one of the Thirty-Six Sages of Poetry and Heijū one of the Later Selection of Six Sixes. Just as the former is associated with *Tales of Ise*, the latter is associated with a work called *Tales of Heijū* or *The Diary of Heijū*.‡ Heijū lived a little later than Narihira, however, and stories like those of the inkstain and of his humiliation by Jijū of

---

*Rōkashō, a 1476 commentary on *The Tale of Genji*.
†Ariwara Narihira (825–880), one of the greatest poets of the early Heian period.
‡*Ise monogatari* and *Heichū (Heijū) monogatari* or *nikki* are tenth-century collections of poem-tales. The latter was discovered in 1931.

Hon'in give the impression that he was something of a buffoon, which Narihira was not. Nor does *The Diary of Heijū* consist entirely of dazzling love stories: the object of his love escapes or politely disposes of him at the end of a great many episodes, and others conclude: "he gave up without a word" or "he decided it was too much trouble and gave up." There are also tales of bungling, such as his relationship with Musashi, a lady-in-waiting to the Seventh-Ward Empress: just when he seemed to have fulfilled his desire for once, he left Kyoto on official business and stayed away four or five days. To make matters worse, he carelessly neglected to explain his absence to the lady. Despairing over his inconstancy, she became a nun.

Of Heijū's many women, the one he loved with the most fervent abandon, the one who caused him to suffer most, the one for whom he ultimately lost his life, was Jijū of Hon'in.

She is called Jijū of Hon'in because she was a lady attendant at the Hon'in Mansion of the Minister of the Left, Fujiwara Shihei, who is referred to as the Hon'in Minister. Heijū was a mere Assistant Commander in the Military Guards at the time, and though he was of good lineage, his court rank was low. He was also a bit lazy. According to the *Diary*, "he found court service tiresome and spent his time daydreaming"—that is, he preferred dawdling to going to work. This angered the Emperor, who punished him by dismissing him from office for a while, though according to one theory the dismissal came as the result of Heijū's rivalry with a superior over a woman. When the woman disdained the other man and yielded to Heijū, the loser in love bore a grudge and slandered Heijū at court. Heijū considered taking Buddhist vows and going into seclusion, and it was at this time that he wrote the poem in Book 18 of *The Ancient and Modern Collection:* "Written when he lost his position," says the headnote. "I see no gates or locks on this sad world—why then do I find it so hard to leave?" He also sent a poem to a lady he knew, a lady-in-waiting to the Emperor's mother: "The cuckoo on Pine Mountain waits for his fate to run out—this is the end, he will cry, and hide himself away." Thus he mobilized the Emperor's mother, and his father, Yoshikaze, appealed to the Emperor; and before long Heijū received a new appointment.

Though Heijū seems to have neglected his attendance at the palace, being averse to work, he often went to call on the Hon'in Minister of the Left. Hon'in was the name of Shihei's residence, north of Nakamikado Avenue and east of Horikawa Street. As the heir to Lord Shōsen—the late Regent-Chancellor Mototsune—and elder brother of the reigning Emperor Daigo's consort, Empress Onshi, Shihei was in a position of unrivaled power and influence. Shihei (whose name should probably be read "Tokihira," but in accordance with a long-standing convention, let us call him Shihei) became Minister of the Left in 899, in his twenty-ninth year. Though he was held in check for the first two or three years by Minister of the Right Sugawara Michizane, Shihei became the most powerful man in the land when he succeeded in toppling his rival in the First Month of 901. At the time of this tale, Shihei was still no more than three or four years past thirty. *Tales of Times Now Past* mentions his "beauty and splendid bearing" and says, "the Minister's face, voice, and manner and even the fragrance of the incense in his robes were wonderful beyond compare," which makes it easy for us to picture an arrogant gentleman blessed with wealth, position, power, beauty, and youth. Hearing the name Fujiwara Shihei, one thinks of the stereotypical wicked nobleman, his face made up in blue, who appears on the kabuki stage in *Kurumabiki,* and so he has come to be seen as a cunning, treacherous man; but this is because people have always sympathized with Michizane—the real Shihei was probably not such a villain as all that. In his study of Michizane, Takayama Chogyū criticizes him for promoting Shihei and thereby betraying the gracious trust of Retired Emperor Uda, who was trying to restrain the Fujiwara clan's high-handedness.* Michizane was, Chogyū says, a spineless crybaby of a poet, and no statesman. It may well be true that Shihei was the better administrator. *The Great Mirror*'s account of Shihei is not all bad: it reports that he had lovable qualities, one of which was the way he would burst out laughing at anything funny and be quite unable to stop.† This attests to a guileless, sunny, broad-minded side to his personality, and there is a humorous episode to illustrate it. Michizane was still at court, overseeing the affairs of state with Shihei, but Shihei would always handle matters by himself and prevent Michizane from participating. A clerk from the Records Office came up with a plan: one day, just as he was presenting a draft document to Shihei, the clerk deliberately farted. Shihei burst out laughing and held his sides. His body shook so much with laughter that he could not take the document; and so Michizane calmly attended to the matter on his own.

*Takayama Chogyū (1871–1902) was a critic who wrote several noted biographies.
†*The Great Mirror (Ōkagami):* a twelfth-century historical narrative.

Shihei was also courageous. It was believed that Michizane's ghost reappeared as lightning after his death to take revenge on the courtiers. One day lightning struck the Emperor's private residence, and all the senior nobles went pale; but Shihei, cool and dignified, drew his sword and glared at the sky. "Even while you lived, you ranked below me, did you not? You may have become a god, but when you return to this world you must respect me!" he scolded. The thunder immediately fell silent, as if fearing Shihei's authority. Thus, says the author of *The Great Mirror,* Shihei did many bad things as Minister, but "he had the Yamato spirit."

This might lead one to think that Shihei was a reckless spoiled brat, but he had another side as well. There is, for example, the story of his plot with Emperor Daigo to discourage extravagance. One day Shihei came to court in gorgeous robes that violated the standards set by the Emperor. Seeing him through the window, the Emperor grew angry and summoned a chamberlain. "Recently we have been strict with those who were extravagant beyond their positions. The Minister of the Left may be the leading minister, but for him to come to court in that extraordinarily gaudy costume is inexcusable. Tell him to withdraw immediately," the Emperor said. The chamberlain nervously conveyed the Emperor's command, unsure what might happen next. Shihei was overawed: forbidding his attendants even to clear the way for him, he hurriedly withdrew and stayed behind locked gates in his mansion for a month. When people came to visit, he would not receive them, explaining, "His Majesty's displeasure is grave," and would not step beyond his blinds. As a result the incident came to be the talk of the town, and people began to abstain from extravagance; but in fact Shihei had arranged everything with the Emperor in advance.

Heijū often called at Shihei's mansion to pay his respects. That very common motive—to curry favor with the powerful in hopes of gaining advancement—was not entirely absent from his thoughts, but another reason for the visits was simply that the Minister and the Assistant Guards Commander enjoyed talking. Despite the vast disparity between them in office and rank, Heijū suffered nothing by comparison in terms of lineage and family, his taste and cultivation were comparable to Shihei's, and both men were handsome aristocrats fond of women. It is not difficult to imagine the topics they enjoyed discussing. Nevertheless, keeping company with the Minister of the Left was not Heijū's only purpose in coming to this mansion. He would always talk with the Minister until late at night, then pick the right moment to excuse himself; but he hardly ever returned directly to his own house. Giving the Minister the impression that he was going home, he would actually sneak around to the apartments of the lady attendants and loiter near the wing where Jijū lived. This was his true objective.

Ludicrously enough, Heijū had been repeating these stealthy visits since the year before—now holding his breath outside a sliding door and thinking: This is the place, now lurking at a balustrade, patiently watching for his chance—but he had suffered uncharacteristically bad luck and been unable to move this lady's heart. Indeed, he had not even been able to glimpse her fabled beauty through a crack in the fence. Nor was it simply bad luck: the lady seemed to be avoiding him intentionally for some reason, and this made Heijū fret all the more. The usual trick in such cases was to win over a serving girl and enlist her to deliver messages. Heijū was not remiss in this regard, but there had been no response to the two or three messages he had sent. Detaining the girl, Heijū would question her persistently. "You did give it to her, didn't you?" "Well, yes, I gave it to her, but . . ." The girl hemmed and hawed, gazing at Heijū with pity.

"And she accepted it?"

"Yes, she certainly accepted it."

"And I'm sure you told her that I hoped for a reply?"

"Yes, I told her, but . . ."

"And then?"

"She said nothing at all."

"Do you suppose she read it?"

"Yes, probably . . ."

The more he questioned her, the more embarrassed the girl became.

One day, after composing the usual detailed account of his innermost feelings, he added plaintively: "I would like to know at least whether you have seen this letter. I do not ask for friendly words. If you have seen this, then I beg you to send me a reply, even if it consists only of the words 'I have seen it.' " The girl came back smiling for the first time.

"Today there is a reply," she said, handing him a letter. Needless to say, his heart was pounding as he raised the message thankfully to his forehead. Quickly opening the envelope, he found that it contained only a small scrap of paper. He looked closely. From the sentence in the letter he had just sent her, "I beg you to send me a reply, even if it consists only of the words 'I have seen it,' " the lady had torn a scrap bearing the words "I have seen it" and put it in an envelope.

Heijū was nonplussed. He had courted many women, but never had he come up against one so spiteful and sarcastic. This was the famous Heijū, renowned for his beauty and accustomed to having women give in to him easily, once they knew who he was; no one had ever treated him so cruelly before. He felt as though he had been slapped in the face. Naturally he made no attempt to go near the lady for some time after that.

For the next two or three months, no longer having any business with the lady, Heijū selfishly neglected his courtesy calls on the Minister of the Left. He did go to pay his respects now and then, but on his way home he would not allow his feet to turn toward those apartments—the "demon's gate" lay in that direction, he would tell himself as he left the mansion and head straight home. Several more months passed, and finally, after a long absence, he spent a rainy summer evening with the Minister. When he emerged from the visit late that night, the drizzle that had been falling at dusk suddenly turned to a heavy rain. To brave the rain all the way back home would be a terrible nuisance, he thought; and then it occurred to him that he might enjoy a different reception if he visited the lady on a night like this. Her behavior that time before, though it angered him to think of it, had after all been a little too deliberate, even for a practical joke. The elaborate means she had come up with to torment him might be evidence that she was interested in him, not that she disliked him. I'm different from those other women (she probably wanted to demonstrate) who get excited the moment they hear your name. She had just wanted to make a point, and now she had made it. Heijū was still vain enough to believe this, which shows that he had not yet learned his lesson or really given up. If he went calling on a pitch-black night in a downpour like this, he told himself, even a woman with a demon's heart would surely be moved. Excited by the thought, Heijū set out in a daze toward the demon's gate.

"Well! I wondered who it might be," exclaimed the serving girl when she appeared in response to his summons. Through the darkness she could barely see him as he stood disconsolately on the boards of the outer veranda, exposed to the rain. "It has been a long time. I thought you must have given up."

"How could I give up? A man's love only grows stronger when he's treated that way. I haven't visited again because I thought it would be rude to be too persistent." Heijū was trying to feign coolness and not look too ridiculous, but as ill luck would have it, his voice quavered so much that even he found it comical. "I have been out of touch, but I've never forgotten her, not for a single day. I've thought of nothing else."

"Have you brought a letter?" The girl's tone suggested that she was not prepared to listen to his whining; all she could do for him was to take in a letter, if he had one.

"I didn't bring a letter. What's the point, if I can't get a reply? Do me a favor, will you? I want to meet her just for a moment—just a glimpse, no, from behind a curtain—and hear her voice. Once I got this idea in my head, I couldn't bear to stay away, and I rushed over here through the rain. She'll take pity on me, just a little, won't she?"

"But her attendants are still awake. It would be awkward right now."

"I'll wait as long as it takes. Until the attendants go to bed. I don't intend to move from this spot tonight until I can meet her," he said forcefully. "All right? Please, I beg

of you. All right?" Gripping her arm, he repeated himself
again and again like a spoiled child. She stared at him,
astonished and frightened by this bizarre behavior.

"Are you really going to wait, then?" she said re-
signedly. "If you are going to wait, I will speak to her after
the others have retired."

"Thank you. I'm depending on you."

"It will be some time yet."

"That's all right; my mind is made up."

"I am only going to tell her that you are here. I can
make no promises about what might happen after that."
Before she went in, the girl said, "Wait outside that sliding
door and try not to let anyone see you." Heijū lost track of
time as he stood waiting. The night deepened; he could
hear people preparing for bed, and finally the rooms fell
silent. Everyone seemed to be fast asleep. Then he heard
someone moving on the other side of the door he was
leaning against, and with a clink the latch was disengaged.

What's this? he thought, putting his hand to the door.
It slid open effortlessly. Aha, he said to himself, tonight
she's been moved to hear my plea. He felt as though he
were dreaming. Shivering with happiness, he stole in and
secured the latch from inside. The room was pitch-black.
He thought he heard footsteps, but no one seemed to be
about; there was only the heavy fragrance of hidden incense filling the room. Feeling his way across the room,
Heijū crept at last to where he thought the lady's bed must
be. Guessing at the spot, he groped around until his hand
touched a long reclining figure blanketed with a silk robe.
The delicate shoulders, the adorable shape of the head—
surely it was she. Her hair as he stroked it was supple, rich,
and cold to his touch.

"You finally agreed to meet me. . . ."

Normally he had a supply of set lines for an occasion like this, but tonight's encounter was too unexpected, and the words would not come to him on the spur of the moment. Trembling all over, he was able to say this much; for the rest, he could only heave hot sighs in her direction, one after another. He clutched her head eagerly with both his hands pressed against her hair, turned her face toward him so he could look at it directly, and tried to make out the features that were said to be so beautiful; but however close he drew her face toward his, he could see nothing through the impenetrable darkness that separated them. After he had peered at her this way for a long time, he finally thought he saw something like a phantom, hazy and pale white. The woman had said nothing through all this and let Heijū do as he pleased. Stroking her face, he tried to imagine its contours with his sense of touch. The woman's supple torso was still limp, and she let him have his way. He could only conclude that she was silently leaving everything to him. But when she felt his body move, she seemed to have a sudden thought.

"Wait," she said, pulling herself away. "I forgot to latch the shōji over there. I'll just make sure it's locked."

"You'll come right back, won't you?"

"Yes, I'll be right back."

What she referred to as a shōji would now be called a fusuma, a sliding partition separating one room from the next. Reluctantly he released her—if indeed the partition was unlatched, they might be interrupted by someone coming in. Rising, she took off her outer silk robe and got out of bed, clad only in an unlined robe and divided skirt. Heijū loosened his clothing and lay down to wait. He was sure that he heard the clink of the latch being secured, but for some reason the woman did not return. The partition was right there; what could she be doing? ... Come to think of it, after the sound of the latch, her footsteps had seemed to move away from him, into the depths of the house, and grow fainter. He sensed that the room was empty.

"Is something wrong?" he said softly. "Hello?" There was no reply. "Hello?" He rose and went to the partition. The latch was open on his side and fastened on the other. The woman had fled to the next room, locked the partition behind her, and disappeared.

Duped again ... Stunned, Heijū stood for a long time in the dark by the partition. What could it mean?—deliberately enticing a person into bed late at night, only to vanish at the critical moment! Even in the past her actions had been too deliberate, but tonight's behavior was the strangest of all. Matters had progressed to this point, and tonight at last his long-cherished love had seemed on the point of being consummated. The sensation of stroking her cold hair and caressing her soft cheek just a moment before still lingered in the palm of his hand. To let her escape when he was only a step away! To grasp a jewel firmly, then let it fall through his fingers! The thought filled Heijū's eyes with tears of frustration. He realized now that he should have gone with her when she rose. His mistake was to assume that everything was all right and to let down his guard. She had probably been taking the measure of his ardor. If he were truly moved by tonight's tryst, he would never have let himself be separated from her, even for a moment. And yet he had let her go by herself while he lay down to wait, and the decision had not pleased her. The moment I show a little compassion (she must be saying), you take advantage. I see that I still have to teach you a lesson. I'm sorry, but a great deal more perseverance is required if you want someone like me as a lover!

Considering the lady's extraordinary perversity, Heijū knew that she was unlikely to come back, but he was not ready to give up hope. Pressing his ear to the partition, he listened for signs of life in the next room. At length he returned to the bed, but he was in no hurry to put on the robes he had discarded there; instead, though he knew he was being foolish, he embraced the robe and the pillow that the lady had left behind, stroked them, and finally lay down, resting his face on the pillow and wrapping himself in the robe. He lay there for a long time.... Who cares if dawn comes? I'll stay here indefinitely. I'll worry about being found when I'm found. She'll have to relent and come back when she sees my determination.... He lay in the darkness with these thoughts running through his head, enveloped in the woman's warm, lingering scent, listening to the desolate sound of the rain and unable to sleep, until the sky began to brighten and voices could be heard here and there; and then, feeling awkward after all, he made a stealthy escape.

Heijū's longing for Jijū grew ever more intense. Pursuing her had been something of a game before, but now he was single-mindedly in love and could not allow his wish to go unfulfilled. To be so consumed with desire was to fall knowingly into the trap she had prepared for him, but he could not stop himself as he was lured, step by step, into doing exactly what she wanted. Finally he could think of no recourse but to summon the girl again and entrust her with a letter. Racking his brain over the wording, he decided to apologize repeatedly for his error that night, using all manner of expressions: I sensed that you were trying to test me, but I forgot myself that night and blundered. I feel the deepest chagrin, because you might point to this as proof that my love for you is not as strong as it should be; but if you can be moved even slightly to take pity on one who has been coming here since last year to see you, undiscouraged by your ridicule, then will you not favor me with just one more opportunity like that of the other evening? . . . The gist was nothing more than this, but it was couched in a variety of telling phrases.

2

MEANWHILE SUMMER PASSED and autumn deepened, and the season arrived for the color and fragrance to fade from the chrysanthemums that bloomed on the rustic fence at Heijū's house.

Celebrated through the ages as an amorist, Heijū cherished not only human blossoms but botanical ones as well, and he seems to have been especially good at cultivating chrysanthemums. "He enjoyed planting gardens around his house and grew many attractive chrysanthemums," says *The Diary of Heijū*. The same section tells of some women who, on a beautiful moonlit night, took advantage of Heijū's absence to steal a look at his chrysanthemums and tied a poem to a tall stem before they returned home.

According to *Tales of Yamato*, Retired Emperor Uda, who was living at the Ninnaji monastery, summoned Heijū one day and said, "Present me with some good chrysanthemums; I think I should like to grow some." Heijū respectfully consented and was about to withdraw, when the Retired Emperor called him back and said, "Include a poem with the blossoms that you bring. I'll not accept them otherwise." Heijū withdrew even more respectfully than before, selected the best chrysanthemums from the profusion in his garden, and presented them with a poem that appears among the autumn verses in Book 5 of *The Ancient and Modern Collection*, with this headnote: "Composed and presented when he was commanded to deliver some chrysanthemums to Ninnaji with a poem attached."

> *Autumn is not the only season for chrysanthemum*
> *blossoms,*
> *For they grow in beauty as they change and fade.**

One winter night, when the blossoms he grew so assiduously had finally lost all color and scent, Heijū called again on the Hon'in Minister and joined him in society gossip of all sorts. Five or six senior nobles were also in attendance, and at first the gathering was quite lively; but finally the others withdrew one by one, until Heijū and the Minister were left alone together. Heijū was anxious to withdraw too, since there was something he wanted to attend to before he went home; but Shihei always started talking about women when he was alone with Heijū, and

*The poem is a veiled compliment to the Retired Emperor, who has aged and moved his residence to Ninnaji.

tonight he broached the subject by asking, "Any harvests recently? You mustn't hide anything from me." Heijū was itching to go, but he had lost his chance to withdraw gracefully, and so for a while they engrossed themselves in the secret stories that only the closest of friends can exchange. Nevertheless, Heijū worried that the Minister must have heard about the recent incident with Jijū; there was no telling when he might raise the subject and needle Heijū about it. Unable to relax, Heijū was on his guard.

"By the way," Shihei said out of the blue. "There's something special I'd like to ask you about." He abruptly left his seat of honor and moved closer to Heijū.

This is it, Heijū said to himself, his heart pounding. Shihei smiled faintly.

"You may wonder what this has to do with anything, but, well, the wife of the Governor-General Major Counselor . . .?"

"Yes?" Heijū stared uncomprehendingly at Shihei's face. The Minister was still smiling.

"You know the Counselor's wife, I suppose?"

"Do you mean . . . his wife?"

"Don't play dumb. If you know her, just be honest and say so."

Seeing Heijū's confusion, Shihei moved even closer. "You may think it strange for me to bring this up out of nowhere, but . . . are the rumors true? That the Counselor's wife is a great beauty? . . . Here, here, I told you to stop playing dumb."

"I am not playing dumb." Heijū was relieved that the topic was not Jijū as he had feared, but someone totally unexpected.

"Come, come. You know her, don't you?"

"But . . . it is not at all as you think."

"That's no good. You may try to hide it, but the cat's out of the bag."

It was common for the two men to go back and forth this way. Whenever Shihei began to tease him, Heijū would stubbornly insist that he knew nothing; and then, as he was questioned more deeply, he would allow that he was not completely in the dark. Questioned still further, he would say, "We only exchanged letters"; then, "I made love with her once"; and then, "Actually, five or six times"; and finally he would admit everything. To Shihei's amazement, Heijū had been in contact with virtually all the famous ladies of the time. Tonight, too, when pressed by Shihei, Heijū stammered some words of denial; but presently the look on his face confirmed Shihei's suspicions, and when Shihei probed even further, Heijū began to open up.

"The truth is, well, I do know a lady who was in the service of the Counselor's wife, and . . ."

"Yes, yes?"

"She told me that the Counselor's wife is an unparalleled beauty and that she is in her twentieth year."

"Yes, yes, I've heard that much myself."

"But as you know, the Major Counselor being such an old man . . . How old is he now? I would guess from looking at him that he must be well past seventy."

"Right. Seventy-six or -seven, I should think."

"That means there is a difference of more than fifty years between him and his wife. Under the circumstances, one can only feel sorry for her. How frustrated she must be, born a great beauty and yet married to a man who could be her grandfather or great-grandfather! Her attendant told me that the lady bemoans her own situation, saying to her women that no one could be as unfortunate as she. Sometimes she weeps when no one is watching."

"Yes, yes, and so?"

"And so? There is nothing to tell; but hearing all this, I, well, you know . . ."

"Ah, ha, ha, ha, ha, ha!"

"I leave the rest to your imagination."

"Just as I thought. I was right, then, wasn't I?"

"I confess."

"And how often have you made love with her?"

"Not so very often. Only once or twice."

"Don't lie."

"No, it's true. . . . I may have met her once or twice, using my friend the serving woman as a go-between, but we never got to be on very intimate terms."

"Well, I don't care about that. What I want to know is whether she's really as beautiful as everyone says."

"I see. Well . . ."

"Well, what?"

"How should I put it?" said Heijū, deliberately tantalizing the Minister. Suppressing a grin, he inclined his head to one side with an air of importance.

The "Governor-General Major Counselor" they were gossiping about was Fujiwara Kunitsune, grandson of the Kan'in Minister of the Left Fuyutsugu and son of Provisional Middle Counselor Nagara. Shihei was the son of Kunitsune's younger brother—Nagara's third son, Mototsune—and thus was Kunitsune's nephew; but as the eldest son of the late Chancellor-Regent Mototsune and scion of the most powerful branch of his clan, Shihei occupied a much higher position. Hence the young nephew, having already reached the important post of Minister of the Left, regarded his dotard uncle the Major Counselor as a subordinate.

Kunitsune, who died in 908 in his eighty-first year, was extremely long-lived for his time, but he was a good-natured man of no special ability who no doubt was able to rise as high as Junior Third Rank Major Counselor only because of his longevity. Having once been appointed Provisional Governor-General of Dazaifu, he was called the Governor-General Major Counselor; but he did not become a Major Counselor until the First Month of 902, in his seventy-fifth year. His only strong point was his extraordinarily good health. We can imagine the extent of his stamina when we consider that at such an advanced age he had a wife in her twenties, by whom he fathered a son. Incidentally, in our own Shōwa period, a famous poet of sixty-seven or sixty-eight experienced "love in old age" with a woman in her forties, providing the newspapers and magazines with material for titillating stories and causing a stir that is still fresh in our memories.* The main topic of conversation among the old poet's friends at the time was whether his physical strength would be up to the task, and one man was curious enough to ask the woman herself about it. When he reported that she felt no inadequacy at all in that regard, we could only marvel at—and envy—the old poet's stamina. If such a couple is unusual enough to excite public interest even in modern times, a man like Kunitsune—eight or nine years older than our old poet and married to a woman fifty years his junior—must have been extremely rare in the ancient days of the Heian court.

*The reference is to Kawada Jun's 1948 romance with one of his students.

The Counselor's wife was the daughter of Ariwara Muneyana, Governor of Chikuzen, and thus she was the granddaughter of the Ariwara Middle Captain Narihira, but her exact dates are not known. It is hard to believe that she was as much as fifty years younger than the Major Counselor, but *Tales of the Generations** says that she was "barely twenty" and *Tales of Times Now Past* that she was "just over twenty," leading to the conclusion that she might have been twenty or twenty-one. The fact that Narihira was her grandfather is not enough to confirm that she was a beauty, but her son, Atsutada, was a handsome man too, and so her appearance probably was worthy of a family noted for its good looks. Shihei had heard rumors to this effect; he had also heard that she occasionally received a lover behind her husband's back and that the lover seemed to be none other than Heijū. If all this is true, he told himself, I can't leave such a beauty to a doddering old man or to that lowly Heijū; it's only natural that I should have her for myself. And just as Shihei was burning with this ambition, Heijū showed up innocently on one of his courtesy calls.

How Shihei finally achieved his wish, deftly snatching his aunt by marriage from his uncle and making her his own, will be explained later. A poem that Heijū is said to have sent her while she was still Kunitsune's wife appears in *Tales of Yamato*:

> In spring fields the clinging vines grow green:
> I would cling to you as my wife—and what think
> you?

Yotsugi monogatari, a collection of tales, possibly from the thirteenth century.

Though it is not clear whether he meant what he said, Heijū's sending such a poem suggests that he must have been fairly serious about the lady. Now, suddenly forced by Shihei to divulge his secrets, he was too flustered to give clear answers; the truth is that he had not been able to get his former lover out of his mind. Being a philanderer, he had had relations with countless women, most of whom he abandoned after one night and whose faces and names he did not remember; but with this beautiful woman— though recently they had drifted apart—he had enjoyed an exceptional relationship for some time. All his attention was on Jijū at the moment, because he found himself drawn irresistibly into pursuing her and she kept him hanging; but this did not mean that he had completely severed his ties with the other lady. And now Shihei's unexpected interrogation set Heijū to thinking about her again.

"As I said before, I met her only once or twice and so cannot be certain," said Heijū, still dissembling. "But yes, I suppose it is true that she is very good-looking." He spoke slowly and with apparent reluctance.

"Hmmm. Then the rumors are true."

"Having come this far, I shall hide nothing from you. I can safely say that no one else has a face quite like hers. I would even venture to say that of all the women I have met, the Counselor's wife is the most beautiful."

"Hmmm," said Shihei, with a sort of groan. For a moment he was still.

"From what you've seen, how is their marriage? I imagine it's not going so well with her and an old man like that."

"Yes, well, at times she spoke of her unhappiness and her eyes would fill with tears; but she also said that the Major Counselor was extremely kind and took good care of her. And so I cannot be sure how she really feels. They do have a cute little boy. . . ."

"How many children are there?"

"Only one, I think. A boy of three or four."

"Why, that means the child was born when the Counselor was past seventy!"

"Yes, it is quite a feat."

Questioned still further on every detail concerning the lady, Heijū willingly told what he knew. Looking back, he realized that he might never meet such an elegant and endearing woman again, but his love for her had largely been fulfilled. He could never say about any woman that he had known the full extent of her charms, that he had exhausted the dreams they shared, that she no longer interested him at all; but he felt more strongly drawn by far to the unknown woman—to the woman who was driven to employ one technique after another in fanning his passion. Such were Heijū's feelings. The psychology of the sensualist is always the same, whether he is an aristocrat of the ancient court or an Edo-period sophisticate: he will not concern himself with a woman he has left behind. Heijū must have thought that if the Minister's heart was set on the lady, he could do as he liked. Also, though others might feel differently, it troubled Heijū's conscience to carry on immorally under the nose of the kindly Major Counselor. Inveterate cuckolder though he was, Heijū felt an uncharacteristic twinge of compassion at the sight of the pathetic old man, thin as a skeleton, who had been lucky enough to find a beautiful young wife and who found total satisfaction in serving her.

By the way, Major Counselor Kunitsune and Heijū seem not to have had much to do with each other, aside from the connection provided by the lady. One autumn, however, a messenger brought a letter on some insignificant matter from Kunitsune to Heijū, and Heijū attached a chrysanthemum bloom to his reply. The story appears in *The Diary of Heijū*, along with the poem that Kunitsune composed and sent to Heijū as soon as he received the blossom:

> *Having passed through many reigns, this old man*
> > *leaning on his staff*
> > *Wishes there were a way to see the blossom's home.*

Heijū replied:

> *Were you to grace this road, the chrysanthemums*
> > *Mingled in a tangle of reeds would surely grow more*
> > *fragrant.*

It is not clear when this exchange took place. Could Heijū, recalling that he had already plucked the old man's most cherished blossom, have intended his gift to be ironic?

✿ SHIHEI now made it a point to greet Kunitsune suavely whenever he saw him at court. It should not be remarkable that Shihei would show respect and concern for an elderly man who was, after all, his uncle, even if he was of lower rank; but Shihei—who had conducted himself more haughtily than ever since toppling Michizane and gloried in strutting before all the other courtiers—had never before paid the slightest attention to his uncle. Now there had been a shift in the wind, and he would display a strange, cheerful smile whenever he met his uncle. He would also offer contrived greetings: I am delighted to see you in such excellent health, but this cold weather must be hard on you; do be careful not to catch cold. One morning when the chill was particularly severe, he saw a drop of mucus on the tip of his uncle's nose. Going quietly to the Counselor's side, he said, "Your nose is wet. . . . When you are cold," he added softly, "the best thing is to wear lots of quilted clothing."

Like so many old people, the Major Counselor was a little hard of hearing. "Quilted . . . ?" he asked.

"Yes, yes," Shihei said, nodding to himself and mumbling something the old man could not hear, and when the Counselor returned to his house, a courier from the Minister of the Left arrived with a huge load of fresh white silk floss. "How I envy you, hale and hearty at the age of nearly eighty and putting much younger men to shame. The nation is fortunate indeed to have such a courtier. Pray continue to look after your health, that you may extend your life on and on." Presenting this verbal message with the gifts, the courier left; but another arrived in the evening two or three days later, after nearly a foot of snow had accumulated since morning. The courier inquired about the Major Counselor's health on this snowy day and reminded him that the night would be unusually cold; and then, holding it up reverently, he carried in a garment box. "This was brought from China," he said. "The late Lord Shōsen used to wear it in the winter, but the Minister of the Left, being young, has no occasion to use it. He wishes his uncle to wear it in place of his father." He left the box with the Major Counselor. Inside the garment box was a magnificent sable robe, the fragrance of incense from an earlier generation still lingering in its folds.

There were many other presents. One day it would be brocades, damasks, and other weavings; another day, rare varieties of aromatic wood, also said to be from China; and another, multilayered robes in purple and red, russet and yellow—whenever an occasion arose, couriers would arrive on one pretext or another in rapid succession. It never occurred to the Major Counselor to question Shihei's motives; he was simply full of gratitude. Anyone reaching a certain age will be moved to tears of joy when a young person says a few kind words, and this was all the more true of the timid, good-natured Kunitsune. Shihei was his nephew, but he was also the greatest man in the realm, destined to become Regent as the heir to Lord Shōsen. That he should remember his flesh and blood and be so attentive to his useless old uncle!

"Yes, it's good to live a long life!" said the old man one

evening as he rubbed his wrinkled face against his wife's plump cheek. "Just having you as my wife has made me as happy as can be, and now on top of that I'm being treated so kindly by a man like the Minister of the Left! . . . Truly, you never know what good fortune might be awaiting you."

Feeling his wife nod silently against his forehead, the old man pressed his face even closer to hers and, with his hands supporting the back of her head, caressed her hair for a long time. It had not been so until two or three years ago, but recently the old man's lovemaking had grown steadily more persistent. In the winter, unwilling to leave his wife for even a moment, he slept with his body pressed tightly against hers all night. To make matters worse, the Minister's kindness had moved him so deeply that he began drinking too much and, crawling into bed drunk, he would entwine his arms and legs with his wife's more tenaciously than ever. Another of his peculiarities was to insist on keeping the lamp burning as brightly as possible. This was because he was not satisfied just to caress his wife with his hands: now and then he liked to draw back a foot or two, the better to gaze admiringly at her beauty, and so it was necessary to keep the room brightly lit.

"Still, it makes no difference what I wear anymore. I want you to have those quilted goods and brocades."

"But the Minister gave them to you, My Lord, so that you would not catch cold."

Since she always spoke softly, his wife had difficulty making the deaf old man understand, and she was naturally reticent with him, especially after going into the bedroom. The couple almost never exchanged endearments in bed; the old man did most of the talking, and his wife would simply nod or, once in a great while, bring her mouth so close that he could feel her lips against his ear as she spoke a word or two.

"No, no, I don't need anything. It's all yours. As long as I have you . . ."

Again the old man drew his face away from his wife's and parted the hair that draped over her forehead, allowing the lamplight to fall dimly on her features. At such times, feeling his gnarled, trembling fingers fondle her hair or stroke her cheek, she would let the old man do as he pleased and close her eyes. This was perhaps not so much to avoid the garish light shining on her face as to escape the old man's voracious stare. Such ardor is marvelous in a man of nearly eighty, to be sure; but the truth is that even this old man, so proud of his good health, had finally a year or two before begun to experience a decline in his physical powers. Worst of all, undeniable proof of this had shown itself in his sexual life. The old man realized what was happening, and his despair made him strangely fretful in love; but the despair came less from an inability to realize his own pleasure than from a feeling that he had wronged his young wife.

"Oh, no, please do not be concerned about that." When the old man opened his heart and said apologetically that he was not doing right by her, his wife shook her head calmly and said that, on the contrary, she always felt sorry for him. That sort of thing is only natural when you grow old, she continued; it is nothing to trouble yourself about. To go against nature and attempt something beyond your power will only hurt you. It would be much better for you to take care of your health and live as long as you can, My Lord, and that will make me happy.

"I'm grateful to you for saying so." Comforted by her

gentle words, the old man found his wife more lovable than ever for the depth of her feelings. She closed her eyes again. Peering at her face, he began to wonder what thoughts really lay in her heart, for it seemed odd to him that a woman as beautiful as she, married to a man more than fifty years her senior, should seem so oblivious to her own misfortune. Not only did he feel that he was cheating a naïve wife; he realized that his own happiness was built on his wife's sacrifice. Gazing at her as he held these secret doubts, he found her face even more mysterious, more enigmatic than before. The old man could not suppress a feeling of pride when he considered that he monopolized such a treasure, that no one but he—apparently not even the lady herself—knew that the world held such beauty. He even felt an urge to show off to someone that he had such a wife. Then his thoughts took a different turn: If her words truly reflect her thinking—if, indifferent to her own sexual frustrations, she sincerely hoped only for her ancient husband's longevity—then how should he repay her kindness? He would be satisfied to gaze at her face until he died, but it would be a pity and a waste to allow her young flesh to decay along with his. Holding his treasure firmly in both hands and gazing at her, he had the strange sensation that he wanted to fade away—the sooner the better—and set her free.

"What is the matter?" Startled to feel the old man's tears on her eyelashes, she opened her eyes.

"It's nothing, nothing," he said, as if to himself, and fell silent.

Some days later, around the twentieth of the Twelfth Month, as the year was drawing to a close, gifts were delivered yet again from Shihei's mansion. "Knowing that the Major Counselor will gain one more year of age next year, drawing closer yet to fourscore, we who are related to him offer our deepest congratulations. We present these trifles as a token of our joy. Please accept them and enjoy a happy New Year." To this oral message the courier added that Shihei would probably call at the Major Counselor's house during the three days of New Year's to offer his personal greetings. "His Lordship says, 'Such a long-lived uncle brings great honor to the entire family. For a long time I have wanted to have a leisurely drink with my uncle, share in his happiness, receive instruction in the art of staying well, and learn from his healthy example; but as the days have passed without presenting an occasion to do so, I have been eager to fulfill this desire soon, and the coming New Year is the perfect opportunity. Also, I have been feeling guilty for my failure ever to offer New Year's greetings at my uncle's mansion. I wish to begin anew by calling at the New Year and apologizing for my past rudeness.' This is what he said. I am instructed also to confirm that he will call during the first three days of the New Year, and to ask for your cooperation." With this the courier departed. The message was an even pleasanter surprise for Kunitsune than the gifts. There was no precedent for Shihei's calling at the Major Counselor's house with New Year's greetings—indeed, such a thing was unheard of in past generations. This generous youth, the Minister of the Left, had not only showered the old man with treasures, because he was the eldest member of the family, now he was going to bestow the honor of a personal visit.... In fact, Kunitsune had been asking himself night and day if there was not some way to repay the Minister's kindness. Though his own house was hopelessly cramped in comparison with the Minister's residence, it had occurred to him to request Shihei's presence at a banquet some evening, entertain him as lavishly as he could, and hope to convey even a tiny fraction of his gratitude; but Shihei was not the sort of man to come to the house of a lowly Major Counselor—it would be pointless to invite him, and the Counselor would be ridiculed as an oaf who did not know his place. Kunitsune had refrained; and now, unexpectedly, the Minister himself had proposed that he be the Counselor's guest.

The next day Kunitsune's house was suddenly alive with the comings and goings of a great many laborers. Only a few days remained before the New Year; promptly hiring craftsmen and gardeners, the Counselor began to prepare the house and the landscape garden for the arrival of his important guest. Inside, wooden floors and columns were polished until they gleamed; mats, shutters, and partitions were refurbished; folding screens and curtain stands were moved about as rooms were rearranged. The steward and the senior lady attendant gave directions—Not there; no, not there, either—as they had each piece of furniture moved and moved again. In the garden, trees were dug up, the lake was filled, part of the artificial hill was removed. Kunitsune himself went into the garden and experimented with various arrangements of trees and rocks. This was a once-in-a-lifetime honor for him; he was blossoming in his old age, and he spared no effort or expense in the preparations.

On the second day of the New Year, a preliminary announcement came from the Minister of the Left; and on the third, a gorgeous procession of carriages and horsemen entered the Major Counselor's estate. Shihei had said that his attendants would be few and unobtrusive, to avoid ostentation; but in fact he had many followers, from Major Captain of the Right Sadakuni and Senior Assistant Minister of Ceremonial Sugane—jesters who always tagged along with him—to courtiers and senior nobles, among them Heijū. It was a little past four o'clock in the afternoon when the guests were seated, and the sun went down shortly after the party began. The saké flowed especially fast that evening; host and guests alike were soon feeling its effects. This was probably due in part to the good offices of Sadakuni and Sugane, who had their instructions.

"We need something more than saké," Shihei said presently, directing his words at the lowest seats. At his signal, a certain Lesser Counselor took out a flute and began to play. Someone joined in with a seven-stringed Chinese koto. The company sang along, beating time with fans. Next, a thirteen-string Chinese koto, a Japanese koto, and a lute were brought in.

"The old gentleman should set an example by drinking more."

"It won't do for our host to hold back like that; the rest of us will sober up!"

"Thank you, thank you," Kunitsune began, with drunken tears in his voice. "I'm so grateful. . . . I've never been so happy in all my eighty years. . . ."

"Ah, ha, ha, ha, ha, ha!" Shihei drowned him out with his distinctive, openhearted laugh. "Enough of that kind of talk. Let's enjoy ourselves, shall we?"

"Right you are, right you are," said Kunitsune. He began to sing at the top of his voice:

> "You press me with wine,
> I do not refuse.

Come, my dear, sing!
Do not be slow to sing! . . ."

An avid reader of the *Collected Works* of Po Chü-i, the old man would always recite from it like this when he got carried away. It was a sure sign that he was feeling his liquor. *" '. . . The girls of Loyang have flower-like faces; Ta-yin of Hunan has snowy hair. . . .' "* Kunitsune had been drinking less in his dotage, but he was fond of saké and could put away any amount. Though he held back at first lest he blunder in his role as host to a distinguished guest, his joy was irrepressible, and his guests were constantly pressing more saké on him. He relaxed and his spirits rose.

"Your head may be like snow, but I envy you for being so vigorous." It was Sugane, Senior Assistant Minister of Ceremonial. "I'm called an old man too, but this is only my fiftieth year. I could be your grandson, but recently I've been feeling weak all of a sudden."

"You're kind to say so, but this old man is quite useless."

"Useless? What's useless?" asked Shihei.

"Everything's useless, but one thing in particular has been useless for the past two or three years."

"Ah, ha, ha, ha, ha, ha!"

" 'Ling-lung, Ling-lung, what shall I do? I've grown so old,' " sang the old man, beginning another poem by Po Chü-i.

The banquet reached a climax as two or three senior nobles took turns dancing. Though New Year's Day is said to mark the beginning of spring, the night was chilly and wintry; but here the party blossomed as laughter, songs, and happy chatter rose excitedly together. Loosening their collars and shrugging off a sleeve of their outer robes to expose the robes beneath, all put aside the formalities and celebrated.

4

✿ THE MAJOR COUNSELOR'S WIFE watched the festivities through the slits in her reed blinds. A folding screen behind the guests had obscured her view at first, but as the party grew livelier and people moved around, the end panel of the screen had gradually been folded in (whether by design or by chance), and now she could see the Minister of the Left head-on. Her view of him was veiled by the blinds, but he sat only three or four mats away and was facing in her direction, his form clearly illuminated by a lamp that had been set in front of him. His plump white face was aglow from drinking; his brows twitched irritably now and then, but his laugh was captivating as his eyes and mouth brimmed with a childlike innocence.

"Magnificent!"

"Yes, a man like that is different, there's no question about it."

Her serving women tugged at each other's sleeves and sighed, trying to elicit a response from their mistress, but she reproved them with a sharp look and pressed herself to the blinds as if drawn toward them. She was surprised to see her disheveled husband, Kunitsune, his voice slurred and thick, uncharacteristically displaying his drunkenness. The Minister of the Left appeared to be just as drunk but was not making a spectacle of himself as her husband was. The Major Counselor reeled from side to side in his seat, and there was no telling what his heavy eyes might be looking at; but the Minister of the Left sat upright in full possession of himself, his dignity undiminished by intoxication. He drank on and on, always from a full cup. Everyone sang Saibara* between instrumental pieces; none could equal the beauty of the Minister's voice and the skill of his phrasing. . . . Such was the impression that Shihei made on the lady and her attendants, but there are no documents to indicate whether he actually had musical ability. Still, his younger brother Kanehira was so skilled on the lute that he was called the "Lute Minister," and his son Atsutada was a master musician, the equal of the celebrated Hakugano Sanmi. Thus it may not have been entirely the ladies' partiality: perhaps Shihei, too, had some talent in this area.

Looking more attentively, the Counselor's wife realized that the Minister of the Left was darting sidelong glances toward her. At first he would look stealthily, his eyes hesitant, and then pretend not to have looked; but as he drank more his eyes grew bolder and he gazed in her direction with a suggestive, amorous expression.

> *"At my gate*
> *A man is strolling to and fro—*
> *He must have something in mind,*
> *He must have something in mind."*

*Court songs adapted from folk songs.

The Minister of the Left put extra force into the refrain, "He must have something in mind," as he sang these lines from the Saibara "At My Gate," then unabashedly turned an imploring gaze on her blinds. She had not been certain that he knew she was peeping at him, but now there was no room for doubt. She felt her face redden at the thought. The delicious bouquet of the Minister's scented robes drifted to her behind her blinds, and so, no doubt, the aroma of her own robes reached him where he sat. And this folding screen—maybe someone had guessed his intentions and moved it out of the way for him. In any case, he seemed intent on penetrating the blinds and seeing into the lady's face with his searching gaze.

The Counselor's wife had noticed right away that another man was glancing furtively at her blinds; he sat in the lowliest seats, far from the Minister of the Left. Needless to say, it was Heijū. The serving women had of course seen the elegant young man as well. They refrained from gossiping about him, in deference to their mistress; but silently they must have compared him with the Minister of the Left and debated which was more handsome. On many nights, in the dim, flickering light of her bedchamber, the Counselor's wife had clandestinely yielded to Heijū's embraces, but this was the first time she had seen him rubbing shoulders with dignitaries in a public setting. Even Heijū was overshadowed by Shihei's commanding presence in this company. He looked like a different person—paltry, somehow, and lacking the charm she had felt when they met in the alluring light behind her curtains. And for some reason, Heijū was moping while everyone else frolicked, as though he alone had no taste for saké.

Shihei noticed. "Assistant Commander!" he called

across the room. "You're down in the mouth tonight. Is something the matter?"

The mean leer of a mischievous child played on Shihei's lips. Heijū glanced at him reproachfully.

"No, not at all," he said, forcing a grim smile.

"But you're not getting anywhere with your saké, are you? Drink up, drink up!"

"Thank you, I have had plenty."

"Then let's hear one of those dirty stories you're so good at telling."

"P-please don't joke like that. . . ."

"Ah, ha, ha, ha, ha, ha! How about it, everyone?" Shihei pointed at Heijū as he looked around the group. "This fellow's a master at telling dirty stories and describing his romantic exploits. Shall we have him perform for us?"

"Hear, hear!"

"We're listening!"

Everyone applauded, but Heijū, seemingly on the point of tears, shook his head and begged to be excused. Showing his malicious grin more plainly now, Shihei said, "Why not, when you're always telling them to me? Is there someone present who shouldn't hear? Shall I share it with everyone if you don't want to—that story you told me the other day?" Stifling a sob, Heijū prayerfully repeated, "Please excuse me, please excuse me," again and again.

The night deepened, but the banquet showed no signs of ending, and the revelry grew wilder. The Minister of the Left began to sing "My Pony":

"She waits for me
On Mount Matsuchi—

> *Go quickly, hey!*
> *I want to see her soon!"*

At the end he rose from his seat and ogled the blinds. Others sang lines from "The Eastern Cottage" and "My House":

> *"Open my door and come in,*
>   *whose wife am I but yours? . . ."*

> *"Abalone, turbot, sea urchins so fine . . ."*

> *"Ri-ra-ra-ra-ri-ru-ro . . ."*

After that, everyone yelled whatever he pleased, and no one listened to what anybody else said.

Kunitsune was falling apart. Barely managing to keep upright in his seat, he was still mumbling the lines *"Ling-lung, Ling-lung, what shall I do? I've grown so old.' "* He grabbed anyone who appeared at his side. "I'm so grateful. . . . I've never been so happy in all my eighty years," he would say, tears streaming down his cheeks. Even so, when the Minister of the Left paid his respects and began making preparations to leave, the Counselor admirably remembered his duties as host and called for the gifts he had prepared—a thirteen-string Chinese koto and two magnificent horses, a chestnut and a bay. They were brought out and presented. Seeing the Minister of the Left stagger to his feet, Kunitsune said, "My Lord, I do not wish to be rude, but you are a little unsteady." He, too, rose precariously. "Let me have

---

*The song is somewhat ribald, as "Matsuchi" is written with characters that mean "waiting breasts."

your carriage brought here," he added, and ordered that Shihei's carriage be drawn up to the covered steps at the front entrance.

"Ah, ha, ha, ha, ha, ha! I may not look it, but I'm all right. You're the one who's pretty far gone." Nevertheless, it seemed that Shihei might be too drunk to reach the carriage, even if it were pulled right up to the balustrade. Taking two or three steps, he fell with a thud on his behind. "This won't do," he said.

"Be careful, sir, you are rather shaky."

"It's nothing, nothing." He started to get up but landed on his behind again. "Well, well, what a sorry sight I make."

"At this rate, sir, you won't be able to ride in the carriage," said Sadakuni.

"That's right, that's right," Sugane chimed in. "The best thing would be to wait awhile, sir, until your head has cleared."

"No, no, that would be an imposition on our host."

"What are you saying? This is a shabby place, but I beg you to stay as long as you like!" Kunitsune was sitting nestled up to Shihei and seemed about to take his hand imploringly. "I'll force you to stay, if necessary. I won't let you go, even if you try."

"Then it's all right if I stay?"

" 'All right' is not the word for it!"

"But if you intend to keep me here, you'll have to provide some special entertainment." Shihei's tone had changed abruptly, and Kunitsune looked at him. Shihei's face, flushed before, had gone pale, and the corners of his mouth twitched nervously.

"The banquet tonight left nothing to be desired, and you've offered me splendid gifts; but I'm sorry to say, it's not enough to keep the Minister of the Left here."

"Your words make me want to crawl into a hole! I have done everything I can do."

"So you say, but—it's rude of me to mention this—gifts of a koto and two horses are not enough."

"Is there something else you want, then?"

"Don't make me say it. You have a pretty good idea, haven't you? . . . Come on, old man, don't be so stingy."

"Stingy? You wrong me, sir! I want to repay you for your unfailing kindness—I will give you anything that would gain your satisfaction."

"Anything! Is that what you said? Ah, ha, ha, ha, ha, ha!" Shihei looked embarrassed as he threw his head back and laughed his usual hearty laugh. "Then I'll speak clearly."

"Please, please."

"If, as you say, you truly want to show your gratitude for my unfailing kindness—if, that is . . ."

"Yes, yes?"

"Ah, ha, ha, ha, ha, ha! Drunk as I am, it still sounds crazy. The next part is not easy to say."

"Please go on . . . please."

"It's something not to be found in my house, or even in the depths of His Majesty's ninefold palace, but only here with you. . . . It's more precious to you than life itself, something irreplaceable in heaven and earth. . . . A treasure not to be compared with a koto and horses. . . ."

"Have I such a thing?"

"You have! Only one! . . . Present it to me, old man, as my parting gift!" Shihei looked the astonished Counselor hard in the eye. "Give it to me to prove that you're not being stingy!"

"Right, to prove that I am not being stingy!" parroted Kunitsune. Stepping to the screen that enclosed the back of the room, he folded it up briskly, reached between the reed blinds, and firmly grasped the hem of the sleeve of the person concealed inside.

"Behold, Lord Minister of the Left. . . . This is the treasure more precious to me than life itself, irreplaceable in heaven and earth, the treasure of treasures, the treasure you will find nowhere but in my house." Befuddled by drink before, Kunitsune stood bolt upright now, suddenly reinvigorated. His words, no longer slurred, rang crisply. In his wide-open eyes, however, a strange gleam arose, as though he had gone mad.

"I give you this present, My Lord, as proof that I am not stingy. Please accept it!"

Shihei and the other senior nobles watched silently, spellbound at the unexpected scene unfolding before them. When Kunitsune first thrust his hand behind the blinds, the reeds swelled from inside and the end of a sleeve spilled out, layered in lavender and shades of pink and clearly visible in the darkness. It was part of the clothing worn by the Counselor's wife, but peeking out of the gap this way, it looked like a surging wave, a sparkling kaleidoscope of dizzying color, or an enormous poppy or peony blossom swaying forth. When half exposed to view, the human-size blossom froze, one sleeve still in Kunitsune's grasp, as if refusing to show any more of itself. Kunitsune gently put his arms around her shoulders and tried to pull her out toward the guests, but in response she tried all the harder to take cover behind the blinds. There was no way to make out her features, since she held a fan before her face; even the fingers that held the fan were hidden inside her sleeve. All that could be seen was the long hair falling from both shoulders.

"Oh!" cried Shihei. As if he had been set free from a

beautiful nightmare, he ran to the blinds, brushed the Counselor's hand aside, and grasped the lady's sleeve.

"This gift, Governor-General, I shall certainly accept. It makes my visit here tonight worthwhile. I thank you from the bottom of my heart!"

"This incomparable treasure has found her proper place for the first time. It is I who must thank you!"

Giving his seat to Shihei, Kunitsune came around in front of the screen. "Gentlemen!" He addressed the nobles, who had been watching these developments with amazement. "Gentlemen, there is nothing more for you here. And even if you wait, I doubt that the Minister will be going soon. Please feel free to take your leave." As he spoke, he unfolded the screen again and positioned it in front of the blinds.

The guests made no move to withdraw, though the master of the house had asked them to go; dumbfounded by the extraordinary events that had been taking place, they were studying their overwrought host, unable to tell whether he was rejoicing or crying.

"Please, take your leave." A murmur arose when the host urged them again to go, but few went directly out. They stood up grudgingly; but most of them, exchanging odd looks, would make a show of leaving, only to stop again or hide behind a column or a door as if reluctant to leave until they had seen the incident through to its conclusion.

What was going on behind the folding screen while the guests' curious gaze was directed toward the blinds it enclosed? . . . When Shihei realized that Kunitsune had passed the sleeve to him and retreated to the other side of the screen, he gently pulled the sleeve toward himself, saying nothing. Then, as Kunitsune had done a moment before, he leaned between the blinds and embraced the blossom-like being. The sweet, faint aroma he had sensed beyond the screen now struck his nose with suffocating force. She still held a fan before her face.

"Forgive me, but you are mine now. Do let me see your face." Shihei gently grasped her hand through her sleeve. Trembling, she lowered the fan to her knee. There was no lamp in the room behind the blinds; the oil lamps burning in the banquet room cast a glimmer, deflected by the screen, through to this side. When he realized that the pale white object glowing in the dim light was her face, which he was seeing for the first time, Shihei felt an indescribable satisfaction that his plan had gone so well.

"Now then, shall we go to my house?" He took her arm abruptly and placed it on his shoulder. Not surprisingly, she showed some reluctance as she was pulled up, but after just a little graceful resistance she rose smoothly.

The people waiting beyond the screen were astonished all over again to see the Minister of the Left, who they had assumed would not be coming out soon, emerge almost immediately with an impressive rustling of silk and a bulky, colorful object resting on his shoulder. Looking carefully, they saw that the object was a high-ranking lady—without a doubt, the person whom the master of the house had called a "treasure." Her right arm resting on the Minister's right shoulder and her face buried in his back, she was so limp she might have been dead, and yet she was walking under her own power. The dazzling sleeves and skirts that a few minutes before had spilled out from behind the blinds now dragged along the floor, becoming twisted and entangled with her floor-length hair. The Minister's costume and her five-layered robes formed one huge, swishing mass as they slowly made their way toward the covered steps at the entrance. Everyone moved quickly out of the way.

"Governor-General! I accept my gift and go!"

"Yes, sir," said Kunitsune, bowing his head respectfully. He straightened up. "The carriage, the carriage," he said. Going ahead of them down the steps, he held up the reed blind at the entrance of the carriage with both hands. By the time he arrived panting at the carriage, Shihei was finding his heavy, beautiful burden almost more than he could handle. In the flickering light of torches held by yeomen and grooms, Sadakuni, Sugane, and others struggled on both sides to lift the unwieldy object into the carriage. As Kunitsune lowered the blind, he said, "Do not forget me"; but regrettably the inside of the carriage was pitch dark and he could not see the lady's face. He was hoping that she might give him at least a word of parting, when the figure of Shihei climbing in after her blocked his view.

Just then, as Shihei followed the Counselor's wife into the carriage, a man moved through the crowd to the carriage. The lady's train draped to the ground from under the blind; the man picked it up and pushed it inside. Hardly anyone noticed that it was Heijū. He had left his seat for a time that night, unable to bear any more; but he must have found it impossible to restrain himself when he saw his former lover being carried off by Shihei. Taking out a sheet of Michinoku paper, he wrote hastily:

> *Like the silent azalea that waits among the crags and*
> *pines*
> *I cannot speak, and therefore love you all the more.*

He folded it up tightly and, appearing out of nowhere beside the Minister's carriage, slipped it under the lady's sleeve as he pushed her train inside the blind.

5

KUNITSUNE was fairly alert as he watched Shihei's carriage, bearing Kunitsune's wife, depart with a large retinue; but the tension eased abruptly when the carriage went out of sight. His intoxication reasserting itself, he collapsed in a heap beside the balustrade. He was about to go to sleep where he lay, face down on the boards of the outer veranda, when his serving women helped him to his feet, led him inside, undressed him, put him to bed, and adjusted his pillow. Unconscious through all this, he fell immediately into a deep slumber. Some hours later, however, he felt a chill at the back of his neck as a draft seemed to penetrate his bedding; and when he opened his eyes, the bedchamber was aglow with a pale, predawn light. Kunitsune shivered. Why was the morning so cold? he wondered. Where was he? Had he been sleeping somewhere other than his usual bed? Looking around, he was certain that the curtains and the bedding and the incense permeating them were those of the bedchamber in his own house, familiar to him morning and evening. The only difference was that he was in bed alone. Like most old people, he awakened early. Listening to the roosters crowing at daybreak, he would gaze at his wife's face as she slept peacefully in the same dim light as this morning, but today only an unoccupied pillow lay where her face should have been. Most important, he had always slept with his body pressed tightly against hers, their limbs intertwined without the slightest gap, their two bodies like one; but this morning gaps had formed at his neck, under his arms, all over, and through them drafts blew. It was no wonder he felt cold.

Why was she not here in his arms, this morning of all mornings? Where had she gone?... As he mulled this over, a monstrous something in the back of his mind gradually, indistinctly came back to life with the brightening morning light, until it finally emerged sharply in his consciousness. He wanted to think of it as a nightmare brought on by too much drink, but as he calmed himself, summoned his memories of the night before, and pondered them one by one, he could no longer deny that they probably were no dream, but reality.

"Sanuki." He called to the woman who would be waiting in the next room. Now in her forties, she had been nurse to Kunitsune's wife; then she married the Vice-Governor of Sanuki and accompanied him to his post, and when he died she fell back on her ties with the lady and came to the Major Counselor's household. She had been in service there for many years now. Since the Counselor thought of his young wife as a daughter, he had at some point come to think of Sanuki as her mother. He sought her advice not only on his relations with his wife but on everything relating to the household.

"Are you awake, then, sir?" said Sanuki, kneeling respectfully by his pillow. Kunitsune's face was buried in his bedclothes.

"Unh," he replied grumpily.

"And how do you feel?"

"My head hurts, and I feel queasy. I think I have a hangover."

"Shall I bring you some medicine?"

"I must have put away a lot last night. How much did I drink?"

"Well, I wonder. . . . I never saw you so intoxicated before."

"Really? Was I that drunk?"

Kunitsune uncovered his face. "Sanuki," he said, changing his tone slightly. "When I woke up this morning, I was in bed alone. . . ."

"Yes, sir."

"What's going on? Where is she?"

"Yes, sir. . . ."

"You'll have to say more than 'yes.' What on earth happened?"

"Then you do not remember last night?"

"It's coming back to me little by little. . . . The lady isn't here now? . . . It wasn't a dream? . . . I forced the Minister of the Left to stay when he was about to leave. Then he said that a Chinese koto and horses weren't enough, he wanted a finer gift, he told me not to be stingy. And so I gave him the woman who is more precious to me than life itself. . . . That wasn't a dream?"

"Truly, I wish it had been a dream."

Hearing a sniffle, Kunitsune raised his head. Sanuki was bent over, covering her face with her sleeves.

"So it wasn't a dream. . . ."

"Excuse me for saying this, sir, but how could you do such a crazy thing, however drunk you were?"

"Don't talk that way. What's done is done."

"But would the Minister of the Left really steal another man's wife? Last night must have been a prank; surely he will return her this morning."

"I hope so, but . . ."

"How would it be if you sent an escort?"

"I couldn't do a thing like that. . . ." Kunitsune pulled the bedclothes over his face again. "That's enough. You can go," he said in a thick voice, almost inaudibly.

Now that he thought about it, yes, he remembered what had happened. It was a crazy thing to do, but he understood the mentality that had led him to it. Thinking that last night's banquet would be the perfect opportunity to repay his debt to the Minister of the Left, Kunitsune had entertained him to the best of his ability; but there were limits to his abilities, and he had been ashamed and frustrated that he could not provide a reception to satisfy the Minister. Just as he was reproaching himself—feeling guilty for offering such a meager banquet, wishing there were something more he could do to please—the Minister of the Left had spoken to him that way and added "don't be so stingy" for good measure. Stung to the quick, Kunitsune had decided to give the Minister of the Left anything he desired. And he needed no hints to guess what it was the Minister desired. All evening, the Minister had been casting amorous glances at the blinds. He had shown some restraint at first, but gradually he grew bolder, until finally, in full sight of the lady's husband, he rose from his seat and ogled. . . . Kunitsune might be decrepit with age, he might have bad circulation, but how could he fail to notice when he was treated as shabbily as that?

Tracing his recollections this far, Kunitsune remembered that his feelings had shifted in an odd direction at that point. Watching Shihei's intolerable behavior, he had not found the rudeness disagreeable: strangely enough, he had felt something rather like pleasure. . . .

Why was he pleased? Why did he feel pride instead of jealousy? He had always considered it his supreme good fortune to have such a rare beauty as his wife; but if truth be told, the world's indifference to this fact left him feeling that something was lacking. Sometimes he wanted to show off his good fortune to someone, to excite someone's envy. This is why he was so pleased to see the Minister of the Left looking enviously at the blinds. Kunitsune was decrepit and would end his days as Senior Third Rank Major Counselor, but he possessed something that this young, handsome Minister lacked. In all probability, the Emperor himself, deep in his ninefold palace, had no one like her in the Women's Quarters. The thought made him indescribably proud, and so he had been pleased. . . . Nevertheless, if it were as simple as that, anyone he might talk to would understand; but in fact he harbored another feeling as well. Over the past two or three years, the decline in his physiological qualifications to be her husband had intensified his belief that to let things go on as they were would be unfair to his wife. He felt more and more keenly the obverse of his own good fortune: his wife's misfortune at having a doddering old husband like him. True, the world held too many women bewailing their miserable fates for one to take pity on each of them; but he had not married just another ordinary woman. Though blessed with enough beauty and refinement to be the consort of the Emperor (not to speak of the Minister of the Left), she had been paired with this incompetent old man, of all people. At first he tried to shut his eyes to her misfortune; but as he came to know and be deeply impressed by her elegance and nobility, he could no longer overlook the enormity of a man like him monopolizing such a woman. He believed himself to be the happiest man in the world, but what was his wife thinking? She would be annoyed, however tenderly he might care for her. Certainly she would feel no gratitude. He could not know what she was thinking, because she gave vague answers to his questions; but might she not wish for the old man's early death, resenting his longevity and cursing his existence?

With this realization, he had another thought: If the right man came along to rescue the pitiable, beloved woman from her unfortunate circumstances and make her truly happy, then he would willingly give her to him. Indeed, that would be the proper thing to do. Because he had not long to live, this would probably be her fate anyway, sooner or later, but since a woman's youth and beauty were finite, the sooner it happened, the better for her. Rather than keep her waiting for him to die, he would henceforth consider himself dead and devote himself to brightening her life. A dead man will watch from the grave over the fortunes of the loved ones he has left behind; he would assume this attitude even as he lived. Then she would understand how selfless his love for her had been. That very morning, she would be shedding tears of gratitude for the old man. She would pay her tearful respects, just as if she were bowing before his grave: Poor old man; how kind he was to me. Hiding out of her sight, he would live out his days watching her tears and listening to her voice from afar. How much happier he, too, would be than if he went on living, cursed and resented by his beloved. . . .

While Kunitsune had watched the Minister's persistence the night before, the doubts that had long occupied a corner of his mind gradually came to the surface as he grew more intoxicated. Was the man really interested in his wife? If so, then the outcome he had been dreaming of so long might come true. If he really intended to bring his plans to fruition, he would never have a better opportunity than this. The Minister had the proper qualifications. Rank, ability, looks, age—on every score, the man was a suitable mate for his wife. This man would be able to make her happy, Kunitsune had thought.

Just as this idea was germinating in Kunitsune's mind, the Minister of the Left had come forward directly. Kunitsune had not hesitated. It moved him deeply that the Minister's wish coincided with his. Now he would be able to repay his debt to the Minister of the Left and atone for his crimes against his beloved. He was overjoyed. In a flash, he had taken action. . . . Even at that moment he had heard inner whispers: Should you be doing this? Aren't you far too generous, however much you want to express your gratitude? When you've sobered up, you'll stamp your feet in frustration at the terrible thing that drunkenness is inciting you to. It's fine to sacrifice yourself for the woman you love, but can you bear the loneliness that will follow? . . . But he had forced himself to scoff at his misgivings: What do I care? What comes will come. If I'm certain that I'm right, then I should act on my convictions, even if I have to borrow strength from saké. Why should loneliness frighten a man who has resigned himself to a living death? . . . And he had let the Minister of the Left grasp the end of her sleeve.

Kunitsune could now identify precisely the motivation for his actions of the night before, but this did nothing to lighten his mood. Slowly burying his face in the bedclothes, he yielded to the remorse that crowded in upon him. What a reckless thing I've done. How could anyone be foolish enough to give his beloved wife to another man, just to show his gratitude? I'll be a laughingstock when word gets out. The Minister of the Left won't thank me; he'll laugh at me. And *she* won't understand that I acted out of love; she'll reproach me for my heartlessness. A man like the Minister could find any number of beautiful women to be his wife, but I'll never persuade anyone to come here, having let *her* go. *I* am the one who needed her most. I should never have given her up. In my excitement last night I thought that solitude wouldn't frighten me, but how bitter the few hours since I awakened this morning have been! If the loneliness goes on like this, how will I bear it? . . . Kunitsune burst into tears. We revert to childhood when we grow old, they say. The eighty-year-old Major Counselor wanted to wail, like a child calling for his mother.

6

TORMENTED by love and despair, Kunitsune lived on for three and a half years after his wife was taken from him. We will touch upon that period in some detail in the section about Shigemoto. Now let us shift the narrative for a while to the subject of Heijū, who tossed the "silent azalea" poem into Shihei's carriage that night.

Like Kunitsune, though not to the same extent, Heijū was left with a bitter aftertaste. The whole business had started that winter night the previous year during a visit to the Hon'in Mansion. Questioned by the Minister of the Left about the Counselor's wife, Heijū had said too much in his enthusiasm. He had only his own indiscretion to blame. Besides considering himself "the greatest amorist of the age," he was a scatterbrain, and Shihei had provoked him cleverly until he divulged everything; but if Heijū had foreseen that Shihei might do anything as reckless as he did, he would not have revealed so much. Heijū had worried that the Minister of the Left (who was no amateur in the ways of love) might make some mischief when he heard about the Counselor's wife; but he comforted himself that the highest minister in the Court—in contrast to a nobody like himself—could hardly go out casually at night, enter a man's house, and sneak into a lady's bedchamber. No, such exploits were much easier for an Assistant Commander in the Military Guards. And so it had never occurred to Heijū that the Minister could do anything as flashy as abducting a man's wife in front of everyone. A wife deceives her husband, a husband deceives his wife, the lovers make unwise plans, cross dangerous straits, and savor a poignant, clandestine tryst—therein lay the fascination of love for Heijū. Exploiting rank and authority to seize a man's possession was naked vulgarity, hardly anything to boast of. Not only did the Minister's outrageous behavior humiliate others and trample on social conventions, it ignored the code of those who followed the way of love and therefore disqualified Shihei as an amorist. These thoughts left Heijū with unpleasant feelings. Though he was lazy, like most men who are much loved by women, he was also easygoing, affable, and disinclined to let things bother him; but what Shihei had done had made him angry as never before.

As we have seen, his feelings for the Major Counselor's wife went deeper than the ordinary attachment, and so their relationship might well have continued had he persisted; but he had tried to forget her by staying away, because, uncharacteristically, he felt sorry for the good-natured old Counselor and was loath to pile up his own sins any higher. Shihei of course knew nothing of these thoughts, and thanks to him Heijū's rare solicitude had gone to waste. Heijū's accumulated sins consisted merely of spending a few secret hours with the Major Counselor's wife; but Shihei, after putting the Major Counselor slightly in his debt, had gotten the old man drunk and, just like that, stolen from him something more precious than life itself. Which case was crueler for the old man—Heijū's or Shihei's? The answer goes without saying. Heijū was angry and frustrated because his former lover had been snatched away beyond his reach to a great man's house; but the ancient Counselor's calamity was not so simple as that. Moreover, the old man had suffered this calamity because Heijū said too much to Shihei. Heijū knew that he himself was the villain who had caused the old man's misery; and the old man remained in the dark about it. Heijū had no idea how to apologize.

But humans are selfish beings. Though he realized that the old man's misfortune was incomparably greater than his own, Heijū felt that he himself had been the unluckiest of all. He was extremely provoked. For reasons we have seen, he had stayed away from the lady and lost interest in her; but in truth he had not forgotten her completely. More precisely, he had nearly forgotten her, but as luck would have it, his waning interest had surged back to life the moment he realized that Shihei was curious about her. After that night the previous year, Heijū had watched uneasily as Shihei began to ingratiate himself with his uncle, the Major Counselor. Wondering what Shihei was up to and suspicious of his motives, Heijū had paid close attention as the affair unfolded. Then there had been talk of a banquet, and he was ordered to go along.

That evening Heijū was in a gloomy mood from the start, having a vague presentiment that something was about to happen. He sensed that the Minister of the Left had a reason for including him in the party. Once the banquet was under way, his misgivings increased when he saw how fast the saké was flowing, when the Minister of the Left ganged up with his henchmen to get the old man drunk, and when the Minister ogled at the blinds and singled out Heijū for a barrage of sarcasm. Seeing the malicious gleam in Shihei's eye, the flush on his besotted face, his shouting, singing, and laughing, Heijū sensed all the more that the lady behind the blinds was in danger. Simultaneously, he felt his love reviving with all its former strength. When Shihei forced his way behind the blinds, Heijū rushed from his seat, unable to bear it any longer; but he could not stay still when he saw the lady being loaded into the carriage. Running up to the carriage, he had tossed the poem inside, scarcely aware of what he was doing.

Heijū rejoined the escort and followed the carriage to the residence of the Minister of the Left, then trudged through the dark streets to his own house. His love increased with every step. He had hoped to catch at least a glimpse of her when the carriage reached the Hon'in Mansion and the lady got out, but his wish came to nothing, and the longing flared up even more intensely when he realized that she was cut off from him forever. It surprised him that he still loved her so much, that his passion for her had not faded; but Heijū's yearning was probably stimulated by the lady's having become a flower on a mountain peak, far beyond his reach. In other words, he would have been able to get back together with the lady anytime he wished while she was still the ancient Counselor's wife, but now it would be impossible. The vexation he felt as a result was probably the principal cause of his passion.

Incidentally, Heijū's "silent azalea" poem appears anonymously in *The Ancient and Modern Collection,* where the line "When I recall the silent azalea among the timeless mountain crags" replaces "Like the silent azalea that waits among the crags and pines." *Summary of the Ten Precepts,** on the other hand, identifies the poet as Kunitsune:

> Lord Shihei must have been an overbearing man in every way. His uncle, Major Counselor Kunitsune, was married to the daughter of Ariwara Muneyana. Shihei tricked his uncle and made the lady his own principal wife. She was the mother of Lord Atsutada. Lord Kunitsune grieved, but he was afraid of what people would say and so did nothing about it.

> *When I recall the silent azalea among the timeless*
> *mountain crags*
> *I cannot speak, and therefore love you all the more.*

*Jikkinshō, a thirteenth-century collection of tales.

It is said that Lord Kunitsune composed this poem
at the time.

This version is more sonorous than the other, and it is
moving to think that old Kunitsune wrote it, but inquiries
of this sort are beyond the scope of this novel. Let us accept
both versions for now. As the passage says, Shihei's objective was to steal the Ariwara lady by trickery, and so of
course he did not send her back to the Major Counselor the
next morning. On the contrary, he lodged her in the main
hall of his house, in inner rooms that he had furnished for
her in advance, and cared for her lovingly. The very next
year she gave birth to a son, the future Middle Counselor
Atsutada, and finally people began to refer to her with
respect as "the Lady of Hon'in." Timid Kunitsune recognized the situation but could do nothing. "Vexed, remorse-
ful, grief-stricken, and desolate," according to the account
in *Tales of Times Now Past,* "he let others think that the affair
had turned out as he wished, but in his heart he longed for
her desperately," and he passed his days in misery. Heijū,
on the other hand, was not ready to give up: he was bold
enough to pay court to the lady—when he could find an
opening—even now that she was married to the Minister
of the Left. The best evidence for this is a poem in Book
II, the third book of love poems, of *The Later Selection.**

Heijū met secretly with a lady in the household of
Major Counselor Kunitsune and together they
pledged their eternal love, but she was suddenly
taken away by the Honorary Chancellor (Shihei)

*****Gosenshū,** tenth century.

as his wife. Unable even to send her a letter, he called to her four-year-old child, who was playing in the west wing of Hon'in Mansion. Show this to your mother, he said, writing a poem on the child's arm.

> *The promises we exchanged so long ago have led*
> *to misery—*
> *What was your pledge, that this should be its only*
> *trace?*

The poem that follows—"Response, author unknown"—is worth noting:

> *With whom did I pledge my love in the waking world?*
> *On a fleeting path of dreams I wander, doubting who*
> *I am.*

It is not difficult to imagine that the complications presented by Kunitsune and Heijū led Shihei to order a strict watch over his new wife and to allow only certain people to approach her, but Heijū was somehow able to get around the precautions, win over the child, and employ him to carry poems. According to *Summary of the Ten Precepts,* the child was "the lady's little boy, only about four years old"; *Tales of the Generations* says that Heijū "wrote on her little boy's arm." The boy was the future Captain Shigemoto, the son born to the Ariwara lady and Kunitsune. No doubt he, and only he, was allowed to come and go freely, accompanied by his nurse, after his mother had been taken to the Hon'in Mansion. Presumably, the shrewd Heijū had been aware of this for some time and skillfully won the child over, so that when he came upon the boy playing one day at the west wing of his mother's Hon'in residence, Heijū promptly recruited him as a go-between. It is easy to picture Heijū loitering about, hoping to get close to the lady, when he had nothing else to do. Perhaps he wrote the poem on the little boy's arm because he found himself without paper when the time came, or because he was worried that paper was more likely to go astray. The Minister's wife wept bitterly when she read the poem that her former lover had inscribed on her son's arm. Wiping the letters off, she wrote her "waking world" poem on the child's arm in reply. "Show this to the gentleman," she said, pushing the child away. Then she hid in confusion behind her curtains.

Apparently Heijū communicated with the lady in this way more than once while her husband, the Minister of the Left, was at the height of his power, for another of his poems is preserved in *Tales of Yamato*:

> *Do you remember the vows that we exchanged*
> *So long ago, not knowing what the future held?*

It seems that the Minister's wife composed a poem in reply to this as well, but unfortunately it has not survived. But, though Heijū was able to correspond with the lady, he was not allowed to meet her. He seems gradually to have lost hope and given up on her, for his relationship with this lady came to a sad end. His sensualist's heart then turned once again to another lover from the past, Jijū. After all, she lived as a lady attendant in the Hon'in Mansion, and Heijū was not about to slink away empty-handed when he realized that he had no chance with the Minister's wife. He certainly did not dislike Jijū and must have thought that he would be disgraced as a man if he did not prevail with her this time. Nevertheless, the extraordinary spiteful Jijū was unlikely to give in to him now, of all times. Had Heijū pursued her single-mindedly before, his ardor undiminished even as she made a fool of him, he would have passed the test and been accepted; but he had been sidetracked, and the lady had lost her temper and grown more perverse than ever. Whatever he said to her, she would turn up her nose and refuse to listen.

Having been robbed of one lover and spurned ferociously by another, Heijū worried about his reputation as an amorist and pleaded desperately with Jijū; but it would be too much trouble to give a full account of the particulars here. The reader should imagine that Jijū, a self-assured woman who took a special interest in tormenting men, must have assigned Heijū more tests like those before, or far crueler, and that Heijū, patiently enduring each ordeal this time, finally, with the greatest difficulty, succeeded in satisfying her pride and gained her acceptance. Though Heijū finally achieved his wish, however, and was in a position to enjoy the trysts that had been his goal for so long, the lady remained as sarcastic as before. One time in three, she was apt to hold him up to ridicule with outlandish pranks she had concocted, and she would stick her tongue out at him or make a face as he turned to go home unfulfilled. Finally the exasperated Heijū would say to himself, This is infuriating! When is she going to stop making a fool of me? Who says I can't give up a woman like that? . . . Again and again he made up his mind; again and again he yielded to temptation. The famous episode that appears in *Tales of Times Now Past* and *A Collection of Tales from Uji** must have occurred around this time. Most readers will already be familiar with it, since apparently it has

*_Uji shūi monogatari_, thirteenth century.

also been introduced in a work by the late Akutagawa Ryūnosuke;* but we will give the gist here, for the benefit of those who have not read it.

Heijū wanted to find some defect in Jijū. She might be a flawless beauty, he thought, but if he could see proof that she was an ordinary human being, he would awaken from the dream that he had wandered so far into and lose interest in her. The idea he came up with was this: However beautiful she was, the matter she expelled from her body would be as filthy as anyone else's. Somehow he would steal her chamber pot and certify its contents. When he realized that he, too, grimaced and produced the same dirty stuff, he would feel an aversion for her at once.

By the way, the author does not know what chamber pots were like at the time. *Times Now Past* has only "a box," but *Uji* refers to "a leather pot"; perhaps it was customary to use a box made of leather. In any case, ladies of Jijū's rank would do their business in a box and have a maidservant take it away to empty from time to time. Hiding near Jijū's apartments, Heijū waited for the servant who handled the box to emerge. One day a charming young woman of sixteen or seventeen appeared. Her hair fell only two or three inches short of the hem of her gauzy robe, which was lavender lined with fuchsia; her red skirt was carelessly hitched up. She had wrapped the box in a cinnamon-colored cloth and held a decorated crimson fan over it. Heijū followed stealthily. When they came to a deserted place, he rushed up and laid his hands on the box.

*Akutagawa Ryūnosuke (1892–1927) is best remembered for his short stories, one of which is "Kōshoku" (The Art of Love), the work referred to here.

"What are you doing!" she said with a shriek.

"Let me have it!"

"What? But this is . . ."

"Don't worry, I know what it is! Just let me have it."

Taking advantage of the woman's confusion, he wrested the box from her and raced away.

Concealing the box carefully under his sleeves, Heijū fled to his house and shut himself up in a room. After making sure that no one else was around, he placed the box respectfully on the dais and examined it from this angle and that. This container, he thought, holds something from the woman I've lost my heart to. He was reluctant to raise the lid. Looking carefully, he saw that it was no ordinary leather case but a splendid, gold-lacquered box. Picking it up again, he lifted it, lowered it, turned it around, and tried to estimate the weight of its contents. When at length he nervously removed the lid, a savory fragrance like that of clove incense struck his nose. Puzzled, he looked inside. The box was half filled with brownish-yellow liquid, at the bottom of which lay three dark lumps, each of them two or three inches long and about the thickness of his thumb. The ambrosial fragrance was not what he would have expected, however, and so he poked a stick of wood into one of the lumps and raised it to his nose. The scent was identical to that of the incense called *kurobō*, made by kneading together aloes, cloves, pulverized shell, sandalwood, and musk.

"Poking the contents, he held a piece up to his nose and sniffed. It had the inexpressibly fragrant aroma of *kurobō*. He was completely baffled. She is not of this world, he thought. Looking at the contents of her chamber pot, he was seized with a frantic desire to be on intimate terms with her." Such is the description in *Times Now Past*. In short, his effort to get over her by viewing evidence that she was just an ordinary person had the opposite effect: he was far from losing interest in her. Still puzzled, though, Heijū drew the box closer and took a tiny sip of the liquid inside. Yes, it smelled strongly of cloves. Then he nibbled a bit of the object he had impaled on a stick. It was both bitter and sweet. He gave the matter some thought as he explored the taste carefully with his tongue. What looked like urine must be a decoction of cloves; the lumps that looked like feces would be a blend of yam, incense, and sweet-grass nectar, kneaded together and pushed through the fat bamboo handle of a writing brush. But when he had figured this out, resignation was more difficult than ever to achieve. What a resourceful woman, he thought, to see into a man's heart and go to such lengths to bewitch him with her chamber pot! She was, indeed, no ordinary person. His love for her only grew stronger.

There is no telling how far a man's fortunes will turn once they begin to go bad. Despite his reputation, Heijū had no success in love after he inhaled the fragrance of Jijū's chamber pot. It was one failure after another for him. To make matters worse, Jijū grew steadily more haughty and cruel: the hotter he became, the colder her rebuffs. When he was almost there, she would push him away. As a result, poor Heijū fell ill and worried himself to death. "I cannot rest until I make her mine, Heijū thought, and bewildered by love, he presently fell ill. Tormented, he finally died," according to *Tales of Times Now Past*. But there is one more point that cannot be omitted. According to *Summary of the Ten Precepts*, Jijū was Heijū's lover to begin with, but Shihei interfered and stole her away. My guess is that since Jijū was an attendant at the Hon'in Mansion, Shihei surely had a relationship with her early on, and Heijū, wittingly or not, had entered into a love triangle. The chamber pot, then, and the many other pranks that Jijū played on Heijū, may have been suggested by the Minister of the Left, manipulating her from the background. If this is the case, then it was Shihei who killed Heijū.

7

I WROTE EARLIER that the year of Heijū's death is uncertain, being given as 923 or 928. The account in *Times Now Past*—that Heijū died of illness, brought on by the Jijū affair—gives the impression that he predeceased Shihei; but the headnote cited above from *The Later Selection* leads one to think that it was Heijū who lived longer. It is clear in any case that Shihei died on the fourth day of the Fourth Month, 909, in his thirty-ninth year, four or five years after he abducted the Counselor's wife.

The Minister of the Left's early death, before he had fully realized his promise, was seen by people at the time as punishment for his many evil deeds, and the curse of Lord Sugawara Michizane's angry ghost was considered the most significant factor of all. Michizane had died on the twenty-fifth day of the Second Month, 903, at his place of exile in the province of Tsukushi. One of Shihei's co-

conspirators in the plot to defame Michizane—Major Captain of the Right and Major Counselor Sadakuni—died in his forty-first year, on the second day of the Seventh Month, 906; and on the seventh day of the Tenth Month, 908, Consultant and Senior Assistant Minister of Ceremonial Sugane, another of Shihei's confederates, died in his fifty-third year. It was said that Michizane's ghost transformed itself into lightning to strike down Sugane. A number of strange tales tell how Michizane took the form of lightning to settle his grudges; here I will relate those that concern Shihei and his family.

Lord Michizane's ghost first appeared on a bright moonlit night in the summer of the year of his death. One morning before dawn, the thirteenth abbot of Enryaku Temple, Hosshōbō Son'i, was contemplating the Three Secrets atop Shimei Peak. Hearing the sound of someone knocking at the cloister gate, Son'i went to open it. There stood the Sugawara Minister, who was supposed to be dead. Hiding his agitation, Son'i respectfully showed his guest to a private chapel and asked why he was being honored with this late-night visit. The ghost replied, Born regrettably into the corrupt world of man, I suffered groundless defamation, demotion, and banishment. In order to have my revenge, I shall take the form of lightning, fly through the sky, and approach the Phoenix Gate of His Majesty's palace. I have already received permission to do this from Brahmadeva, the Four Devas, Yamarāja, Śakradevānāṁ Indra, the Judges of the Five Paths, the Commanders, and the Bursars. I need defer to no one. Nevertheless, Your Reverence has great virtue in the Dharma. More than anything else, I fear being subdued by your religious powers. When the time comes, I beg that you will recall the vows you and I made as priest and benefactor and decline any summons from His Majesty's court. I have come all the way from Tsukushi tonight in my desire to say this to you.

Son'i replied, I sympathize with your complaint, but there have been many instances since ancient times of wise men suffering misfortune at the hands of small men. It is not your fate alone, and the world is unjust. Your resentment is shameful; I wish that you would abandon these thoughts. Still, I am mindful of the deep bond between us over these many years. If it truly is your wish, I shall do as you say and decline a message from the Emperor, even if it means that my eyes are plucked out. Nevertheless, the entire realm is the Imperial domain, and this lowly monk is an Imperial subject. Accordingly, if there are repeated messages, I shall decline the first two, but I will have no choice but to honor the third. Hearing this, the Minister's ghost made a terrifying face. Son'i said, You must be thirsty, sir, and offered him a pomegranate. The Minister accepted it, chomped it fiercely to bits, and spat out the pieces at the base of the door, where they blazed up in a streak of flame. Son'i made the Water-Pouring Mudrā, whereupon the flames instantly went out.

Black clouds soon spread over the capital, and a violent thunderstorm struck, whipping the wind, flinging down hail, and hurling thunderbolts into the palace. The terrified courtiers scurried under verandas, hid inside clothes chests, or held straw mats over their heads, weeping. Some chanted the *Kannon Sūtra*. It was in the midst of this that Shihei brandished his sword resolutely, faced the sky, and scolded the thunder. But the wind and rain continued and finally caused the Kamo River to flood. Having received three messages from the Emperor, Hosshōbō Son'i reluctantly went to the palace, quieted the lightning with the power of the Dharma, and dispelled the Emperor's troubles. When Son'i's carriage reached the banks of the Kamo River on that occasion, the waters parted and allowed the carriage to cross. It is also said that when Son'i was reciting spells and incantations in the palace, the Emperor dreamed of Acala surrounded by flames and lifting his voice in incantations; and when His Majesty awoke, he realized that it had been Son'i's voice reciting the sūtras.

Son'i's powers may have lost their effect with repetition, however, because five years later, in the Tenth Month of 908, the courtier Sugane was killed by a bolt of lightning. In the Third Month of 909 Shihei began to feel ill and took to his bed. Michizane's angry ghost appeared frequently at his bedside, uttering curses. Yin-yang masters and physicians were summoned; all sorts of incantations, medical treatments, and moxibustion were tried, but to no avail; it became simply a matter of waiting for death. The entire household was beside itself with grief. There was nothing for them to do but call in a holy man of the highest virtue and rely on his powers. For this purpose, no one at the time equaled the celebrated priest Jōzō. Jōzō was the eighth son of Professor of Letters Miyoshi Kiyoyuki, who years before—in 900, when Michizane, as Minister of the Right, was still vying with Shihei for advancement—had submitted a document to Michizane containing the lines: "Li Chu cannot see the dust on his eyelashes, despite his clear vision; Confucius cannot know what is in the box, despite his wisdom." He warned in this document that Lord Michizane would meet with disaster in the coming year and hinted that the Minister should resign his position immediately and attend to the arts of self-preservation. Jōzō's mother was a granddaughter of Emperor Kōnin. Incomparably wise and quick-witted as a child, Jōzō read the Thousand-Character Classic in his fourth year, sought to take Buddhist vows in his seventh, and, discovered in his twelfth year by Retired Emperor Uda, became Uda's disciple in Buddhism. Later, the Retired Emperor commanded him to ascend Mount Hiei and be ordained, and had him study Esoteric Buddhism with Master of Discipline Genshō. Gifted both intellectually and artistically, he mastered not only Esoteric and Exoteric Buddhism but, it is said, more than ten other arts and disciplines as well: medicine, astronomy, Sanskrit, physiognomy, music, Chinese literary composition, divination, soothsaying, navigation, painting, exorcism, and reciting the *Lotus Sūtra*. It is also said that no one equaled him as a performer of music and the other arts. Responding to a summons from the Minister of the Left's household, he found the mark of death already on Shihei's face. He told Shihei that his fate was determined and would be difficult to escape; even if Jōzō employed his various skills, Shihei's chances of surviving would be less than one in ten thousand. The patient, his attendants, and his family nevertheless pleaded with Jōzō, and, unable to refuse, he applied himself to his spells and incantations. His father, Kiyoyuki, had called to ask after Shihei's health and was sitting at the bedside. As Jōzō fervently continued his prayers, a green dragon emerged from both of the patient's ears and spat flames from its mouth. Addressing Kiyoyuki, it said, Because I did not take your hint while I was still alive, I suffered banishment and roamed the skies of Tsukushi, there to end my days in vain. Now, with the permission of Brahmadeva and Śakradevānām Indra, I have transformed myself into lightning and am seeking revenge on those who tormented me. I never expected that your own son Jōzō would interfere and try to subdue me with the power of the Dharma. I beg you to have Priest Jōzō desist.... Awestruck, Kiyoyuki ordered Jōzō to stop his incantations immediately. The moment Jōzō left the sickroom, Shihei expired.

Retired Emperor Uda was furious when he heard that Jōzō, his own disciple, had left the mansion of the Minister of the Left without completing his incantations. Having incurred the Imperial displeasure, Jōzō prudently confined himself for three years in the Shuryōgon'in at Yokawa, where he spent his days in ascetic training; but most people thought it only natural that Shihei died as he did, and few had any sympathy for him. The retribution extended to Shihei's descendants as well. The eldest of his three sons, the Hachijō Major Captain Yasutada, died on the fourteenth day of the Seventh Month, 936, in his forty-seventh year; and the third son, Middle Counselor Atsutada—the child of Shihei's new wife, the Ariwara lady—died on the seventh day of the Third Month, 943, in his thirty-eighth year. Perhaps Yasutada's death in his forty-seventh year should not be called premature for the time, but his was no ordinary death. It is said that he worried about Michizane's curse so much that he fell ill. He summoned an exorcist to his bedside and had him recite the *Sūtra of the Master of Healing*; but when the exorcist came to the line about the Crocodile General, Yasutada thought he heard "choke and die" instead of "Crocodile." He fainted in convulsions and never regained consciousness. Shihei also had a daughter, who became Emperor Uda's Junior Consort and was called the Kyōgoku Lady of the Bedchamber; she, too, was short-lived. Shihei's grandson—Prince Yasuyori, the child of

Shihei's daughter, Jinzenshi, and Emperor Daigo's Heir Apparent, Prince Yasuakira—was named Crown Prince upon Prince Yasuakira's passing, but passed away himself on the eighteenth of the Sixth Month, 925, in only his fifth year. The one exception is Shihei's second son, the Tominokōji Minister of the Right Akitada, who died in his sixty-eighth year, on the twenty-fourth of the Fourth Month, 965. A virtuous man, who always held Michizane's spirit in awe, he went into the garden every night and bowed in reverence before a shrine dedicated to Michizane. Conducting himself with gravity and taking frugality as his main principle, he occupied the post of Minister for six years; but whether at home or away, he never observed ministerial formalities. When he left home, he hardly ever used outriders, dispensed with the usual four footmen, and always rode in the rear of his carriage. Avoiding luxurious utensils when he ate, he put his food on unglazed earthenware, which he placed on a tray resting directly on the floor mat, without a table. Instead of using a pitcher and basin for washing, he had a shelf built at the main entrance to his house, where he placed a bucket and a ladle. A servant would simply fill the bucket with hot water every morning, and when Akitada needed to wash his hands, he would ladle the water himself so as not to trouble anyone. Because he was this sort of person, he rose as high as Minister of the Right and was granted Senior Second Rank. Those of his grandchildren who entered monasteries—Shin'yo of the Mii Temple and Fukō of the Kōfuku Temple—were blessed with security and good health and reached the positions of Major Bishop and Provisional Archbishop, respectively. Another who became a monk was Bodaibō Monkyō of Iwakura, son of Assistant Commander of the

Military Guards of the Right Sukemasa and grandson of Middle Counselor Atsutada. All of these men were able to avoid disaster by embracing Buddhism, but the posterity of Shihei, Lord Shōsen's eldest son, never flourished. It was Shōsen's fourth son, Tadahira, who finally became Junior First Rank Regent-Chancellor; moreover, everyone in his family held prominent positions. It is said that this was because Tadahira, Major Controller of the Right at the time of the banishment, had secretly disagreed with his elder brother Shihei and sympathized with Michizane; sending a steady stream of letters to Michizane in exile, he had formed a close friendship with him.

Shihei's third son, Atsutada—referred to as the Hon'in Middle Counselor, the Biwa Middle Counselor, and the Tsuchimikado Middle Counselor—was one of the Thirty-Six Sages of Poetry and is well known as the author of the poem that begins "My heart since meeting you," in *One Hundred Poets, One Hundred Poems.** "This Middle Counselor was the child of the Hon'in Minister by his wife, the Ariwara lady. About forty years of age, he was extremely beautiful in manner and appearance. He was also of good character and was extremely well thought of in society." As this account in *Tales of Times Now Past* indicates, Atsutada was gentle and agreeable, unlike Shihei. He was also a sensitive, passionate poet who had inherited some of the qualities of his mother's grandfather, Narihira. According to *Evening Conversations on One Hundred Poets, One Hundred Poems,†* the Ariwara lady was already carrying Atsutada when Shihei abducted her from Kunitsune's mansion, so

*Hyakunin isshu, thirteenth century.
†Hyakunin isshu issekiwa (1833), by Ozaki Masayoshi (1755–1827).

that Atsutada was actually Kunitsune's offspring; but since he was born after the lady moved to Hon'in, he was reared as Shihei's child. If this is true, then Atsutada was Captain Shigemoto's full younger brother. The author of *Evening Conversations* does not give his source for this account, but perhaps rumors were circulating at the time. After Atsutada's untimely death in 943, Hakugano Sanmi became indispensable to concerts at the Imperial Palace; if Sanmi was unable to attend, the concert would be canceled. Old men grieved when they heard this, saying that there were no great musicians left, that Hakugano Sanmi had not been so esteemed while Middle Counselor Atsutada was still alive. This story serves as a reminder that Atsutada's death was mourned and that he excelled in music as well as in poetry.

While he was still only a Lesser Captain of the Left Bodyguards, Atsutada was pressed into service carrying morning-after letters between Crown Prince Yasuakira and Consultant Fujiwara Harukami's daughter, who had become the Prince's Lady of the Bedchamber. After the Prince passed away the Lady pledged her love to Atsutada, who was extremely fond of her. One day he told her, "My entire family is short-lived, and I doubt that I shall live very long myself. After I die, you will probably be Funnori's." Funnori, Minister of Popular Affairs and Governor of Harima, was steward in Atsutada's household. "Not very likely!" replied the Lady of the Bedchamber. "No, I'm sure I'm right," Atsutada said. "I'll be watching you from above." It turned out as he prophesied. One can deduce from the example of Yasutada that Shihei's children and grandchildren were so nervous about Michizane's curse that they never had a moment of peace. Atsutada, too, had privately resigned himself, knowing that he was not destined to live long.

Atsutada had a number of other lovers besides the Lady of the Bedchamber. Most of the verses in *The Atsutada Collection* are love poems. In particular, there are many exchanges with Princess Gashi, High Priestess of the Ise Shrine, which gives the impression that their relationship lasted a very long time. Book 13, the fifth book of love poems, of *The Later Selection* contains a verse composed by Atsutada when the Princess went to Ise, having been appointed High Priestess. It bears this headnote:

He set his heart on the Nishi-Shijō Former High Priestess while she was still a princess. The morning after she was chosen as High Priestess, he attached a branch of a sacred tree to this poem and had it delivered to her:

Even if one searched the long seashore at Ise
What shells are to be found there now?

There was also the daughter of the Ononomiya Minister of the Left Saneyori, whom Atsutada called "Mistress of the Wardrobe." He loved her for a long time, but meeting her was difficult. On the last day of the Twelfth Month he sent this:

In love I did not see the days and months go by,
and now
I hear the year will end today.

Her father, the Minister of the Left, got wind of the relationship and made it harder than ever for them to meet. Atsutada wrote this and sent it to her:

How I love you—that much at least
I wish I could say without a messenger.

He also exchanged pledges with a woman named Ukon, a daughter of the Suenawa Lesser Captain, while she was still in service at the Imperial Palace; but he abruptly stopped visiting her when she resigned her post and returned to her family. She wrote to him:

I hear that he lives, who pledged never to forget.
I wonder where the words that he uttered have gone?

Instead of writing a reply, he sent her a pheasant. She wrote to him again:

More cautious than the morning pheasant, avoiding the hunter
*   as it rises*
*   On Mount Kurikoma, I had not thought to be captured by*
*   you again.*

The Atsutada Collection mentions three other women as well: Consultant Minamoto Hitoshi's daughter, who was the mother of Atsutada's eldest son, Sukenobu; someone referred to as his "first wife"; and a woman called "Sukemasa's mother." But it is not clear whether they correspond to any of the women mentioned earlier. Sukemasa, Atsutada's second son, is to be distinguished from the Sukemasa who is ranked with Kōzei and Tōfū as a great calligrapher. According to *The Atsutada Collection*, Sukemasa's mother died giving birth to him, and he was placed with his aunt. His childhood name was "Azuma." Atsutada went to see him in his second year. Weeping profusely, he composed this poem:

Before we could speak our hearts, we parted—
And my keepsake of her is Azuma.

Azuma—Sukemasa—later took Buddhist vows, as we have
seen.

8

ABOVE is a rough account of what befell Heijū,
Shihei, and Shihei's descendants after the abduction.
What became of the pitiful old Major Counselor and of
Shigemoto, his son by the Ariwara lady?

Kunitsune had three sons in addition to Shigemoto.
*Lineages Noble and Base** lists them in this order: Shigemoto,
the eldest; Toshimitsu, second; Tadamoto, third; and
Yasunobu, fourth. Tadamoto's mother is identified not as
the Ariwara lady but as the daughter of a certain Governor
of Iyo. Tadamoto's line continued for many generations,
but neither Toshimitsu nor Yasunobu had any offspring,
and there is no indication of who their mother was. If
Shigemoto was about four at the time of the incident, he
must have been born when the Major Counselor was in his
seventy-second or seventy-third year. Could Kunitsune
have begotten three more children or remarried between

*Sonpi bunmyaku, compiled in the fourteenth century.

then and his death in his eighty-first year? Or is the order in *Lineages Noble and Base* wrong? Could Toshimitsu and the other two have been bastards born before or at about the same time as Shigemoto? For that matter, Kunitsune must have been married to someone else before he took the Ariwara lady, fifty years his junior, as his wife. Was his first wife childless? There are no clues now to cast light on these questions. *Lineages Noble and Base* gives Shigemoto's title as Junior Fifth Rank, Upper Grade, Lesser Captain of the Left Bodyguards, and indicates that he had three sons—Sukeaki, Masaaki, and Tadaaki; but the sons' mother is not identified, and none of the three had any progeny. Further, since Shigemoto's name does not appear in *Appointments of Senior Nobles*, it is unclear when he attained Junior Fifth Rank or when he became a Lesser Captain in the Left Bodyguards; and there is no way of knowing the dates of his birth and death. In addition to *Lineages Noble and Base*, there is an entry relating to Shigemoto in *Tales of Yamato*:

To Lesser Captain Shigemoto, from a lady:

> *A life that died for love—should anyone remember*
> *And come to ask, tell him that I am no more.*

The Captain's reply:

> *Tell at least her corpse that I have come—our dewlike*
> *bodies*
> *Were pledged to fade together.*

The Later Selection, Book II (the third book of love poems), includes this:

Fujiwara Shigemoto visited a lady one night and had her pledge that she would surely meet him again. The next morning he sent to her:

Those pledges we made, calling on the gods—
Oh, dream! refute not our words so ominously.

These references are commonly known; but there is another, which is not so widely read, a manuscript in the collection of the Shūkokaku Library called *Shigemoto's Diary*. It is a partial text, and though there seem to be two or three manuscripts in other collections, the full text has not survived anywhere. Only fragments remain, apparently written sporadically over a period of seven or eight years, beginning with the spring of 942. Shigemoto's yearning for his mother fills their pages.

As the reader knows, Shigemoto's mother was also the mother of Atsutada. How long did she live? We know from the headnote to a poem by Minamoto Kintada in Book 5 (the section containing congratulatory poems) of the *Collection of Gleanings** that Middle Counselor Atsutada held a celebratory banquet for his mother, which we can assume was probably in celebration of her fiftieth year, and in *Shigemoto's Diary* we see that she was still living in 944, the year after Atsutada's death. This would have been thirty-five years after the death of her second husband, the Honorary Chancellor Shihei; she would have been around sixty, and Shigemoto would have been in his forty-fourth or forty-fifth year. Unable to forget his mother even at that age, Shigemoto had good reason now and then to recall her face and long for her. Many years before—at the time of

Shūishū, early eleventh century.

the incident, when he was a child of four or five—he had been allowed to visit the Hon'in Mansion, but the rules of this sad world prevented him from doing so after he had turned six or seven. Thereafter, though he heard that his mother was in good health, he had no opportunity to meet her privately. Anyone who vaguely remembered seeing his mother when he was very young and who lost her when she went off with another man would feel an uncommon longing for her. This would be all the more likely if she had been an exceptionally beautiful woman; all the more likely if he cherished unusual memories, such as visiting her—now another man's wife—just as he began to understand things and having her write a poem on his arm; and all the more likely if he knew that she was still alive. In this light, it is reasonable to view *Shigemoto's Diary* as a text written out of love for his mother. Only fragments remain, but the sections that have not survived would surely have been filled with the same nostalgia for her. Indeed, Shigemoto may never have considered writing anything of this sort until he reached his early forties and his love for his mother had grown more acute than ever. Though it is called a diary, it might also be described as a tale that begins with an account of sad childhood memories—his mother's departure when he was very young, his father's death—and relates the events that led to an unexpected reunion with his mother forty years later, when he visited the site of the late Atsutada's villa at Nishi-Sakamoto, on a spring evening in the mid-940s.

From his diary it would seem that Shigemoto retained fragmented memories of his mother, going back to his fourth year or so, but the earliest ones are no more than vague traces, as pale as the spring haze. He remembers nothing of the events of that night, the most momentous of his life and in the life of his father, Kunitsune—the night when his mother was taken away by the Hon'in Minister—he had simply heard from someone, at some point, that his mother no longer lived in his house. This made him very sad, and he had cried. The person who informed him must have been either the old woman Sanuki or his nurse, Emon. In those days he always slept in his nurse's arms. At her wits' end in the face of his unceasing crying and calling his mother's name, she said, "There, there, be a good boy and go to sleep. Your mother is not here, but she is not so very far away. If you are good, we shall certainly take you to see her."

This made little Shigemoto inexpressibly happy. "When?" he asked.

"Soon," she said.

"Do you promise?"

"I promise."

"Promise . . . promise? You're not making it up, are you?"

Though he repeated this interrogation almost every night as he was put to bed, he suspected in his child's heart that, whatever she might say, his nurse was only trying to pacify him; but it seems that the nurse did speak to Sanuki, because one day Sanuki took him by the hand to see his mother. Early childhood memories are tenuous things, and for some reason he was quite unable to recall that precious day. His memory was fragmented, like old motion-picture film, with frozen images of disconnected scenes, some of them dim, some eerily sharp, lingering in his imagination; and of these many images, one that still came to mind often was of his own childish form at the Hon'in Mansion, sitting by the balustrade of an elevated passageway, gazing idly at the garden.

He knew that his mother lived in the main hall, at the far end of the passageway, and he had been told to wait there until he could meet her. After he had waited awhile, Sanuki would emerge and signal him to come with her. His mother hardly ever let herself be seen near the veranda; she stayed shut up in a room toward the back of the central chamber. When he went to her, she never failed to take him on her lap, stroke his head, and press her cheek to his; and he would say, "Mother."

"My child," she would say, and hug him tightly. But that was all; she would offer a few gentle words, but she never had a serious talk with him, perhaps because he was too young to understand anything she might have said. Eager at such times to memorize the face of the mother he met so rarely, he would look up as she held him; but sadly the room was dark, and the rich sidelocks falling forward veiled the contours of her face. It was like peering reverently at an image of the Buddha ensconced deep in a shrine, and he never had a full, satisfying look. He knew from listening to the gossip of the serving women that there were few women as pleasing in appearance as his mother, and he supposed that "beautiful" must refer to a face like this, but he was not totally convinced that it was so. It felt good, that was all, to be held silently in his mother's firm embrace, because her robes were scented with an especially sweet incense. Even after he had gone back home, the fragrance would cling to his cheeks, to the palms of his hands, and to his sleeves for two or three days, making him feel as though his mother were there, pressing against his body.

The first time the child truly thought of his mother as beautiful was when Heijū accosted him and wrote a poem on his arm. It must have been a spring day, as the buds of a red plum had begun to open near the eaves of the passageway. Shigemoto was playing with two or three girls on the veranda of the west wing when a man came up to him, smiling.

"Hello . . . have you already seen your mother?" He rested a hand on Shigemoto's shoulder.

"Not yet," Shigemoto was about to say, but unsure whether he ought to say so, he kept quiet and looked up at the man's face. Only later did he learn that it was Heijū, but even at the time the man was not a total stranger. Shigemoto had often seen his face before.

"Not yet?" The man could guess from Shigemoto's anxious fidgeting. Conscious of their surroundings, he leaned over and put his mouth to Shigemoto's ear.

"You're a good boy, a very good boy," he said. "I'm sorry to trouble you, but if you're going to see your mother, there's something I'd like to ask you to do for me. . . . You'll help me, won't you?"

"What is it?" Shigemoto asked.

"Just a moment." Putting an arm around Shigemoto's back, Heijū led him a short distance away from the girls. "I have a poem for your mother. Will you deliver it for me?"

Shigemoto had been warned by Sanuki and his nurse that his meetings with his mother were secret; he must tell no one of them. He hesitated, at a loss how to reply. Using different words each time, the man assured him again and again that there was no need to worry, he knew the boy's mother well, she would be pleased if the boy acted as a go-between. He added after every few words that

Shigemoto was a good boy who would listen to reason. He forced a smile and spoke coaxingly at first, determined not to upset the child, but as he continued his expression grew serious, and soon he was trying his utmost to win the boy's assent. Shigemoto realized this. An adult's face at such times can be frightening to a child, and Shigemoto did feel a bit intimidated and apprehensive; but the face also showed signs of an imploring, love-stricken attitude that could not help but arouse the sympathy even of a child.

When Shigemoto nodded his assent, the man repeated, "Good boy, good boy," and looked around cautiously. Taking Shigemoto by the hand, he pulled him into a room and behind a folding screen. There he took a writing brush from the desk and moistened it on the inkstone. "Hold still now, please," he said, folding Shigemoto's right sleeve up to the shoulder. After some deliberation, he wrote a poem in two lines on the child's forearm, from the elbow to the wrist.

After he had finished writing, he held the arm as he waited for the ink to dry. This made Shigemoto think that something else was going to be done to him, but when the ink was dry the man carefully lowered the sleeve.

"There. Now show this to your mother, if you please, when no one else is about. . . . All right? Do you understand?"

Shigemoto nodded.

"Just to your mother, all right?" the man repeated. "Please don't let anyone else see it."

After that, Shigemoto must have waited as usual in the passageway for Sanuki's signal and then gone in to his mother. His memory was faint on that point; but when he had gone behind her curtains and was settled on her lap and in her arms, he said, "Mother," and folded up his sleeve to show her. His mother seemed to grasp the situation at once, but the room was dark, and so she pushed a curtain aside to let in some light from outside. Easing the child from her lap, she held his arm to the light and read it over and over again. Shigemoto thought it strange that his mother seemed to understand everything without asking him who had done the writing, who had come to him for help. Something fell glistening before his eyes. When he looked up questioningly, his mother was gazing into the darkness, her eyes full of tears. It was at this moment that he truly thought his mother beautiful: a reflection of the spring sunlight had floated directly across her face just then, bringing into sharp relief the contours that he had seen before only in deep, dark interiors. When she realized that the child was watching her, his mother hurriedly pressed her face close to his. Now he could see nothing at all, but in recompense the teardrops clinging to her eyelashes felt cool on his cheeks. This moment was the only time in his life that Shigemoto ever saw his mother's face clearly. The image of her features at that instant, and the impact of their beauty, were burned into his mind, never to fade for the rest of his life.

Shigemoto could not remember how long his mother kept her face pressed against his, whether she was crying during that time, or whether she was thinking. Finally she had one of her women bring a pitcher of water and rubbed the letters off Shigemoto's arm. The woman was about to rub them off, but Shigemoto's mother stopped her and did it herself. She seemed to work reluctantly, studying each graph, one by one, as she erased it, as if to engrave the words on her mind. Then, just as Heijū had done, she folded up her child's sleeve, and holding his arm with her left hand, she traced a new inscription, about the same length as the one it replaced.

No one else had been present when Shigemoto first showed his arm to his mother, but two or three serving women had appeared in the meantime, and Shigemoto worried about what Heijū had said to him; but apparently his mother had taken the women into her confidence and told them everything. He clearly remembered his mother writing on his arm but had no recollection of what she might have said to him. Perhaps, he thought, she did these things without saying anything at all.

"Young master," said Sanuki, when his mother had finished writing. He had not seen her come in. "Show your mother's poem to that gentleman. He will be waiting where you left him. Go quickly now and see."

Sure enough, when Shigemoto returned to the west wing, the man was waiting for him eagerly at the veranda.

"Ah! Did she send a reply? Good boy, good boy," he said excitedly, pouncing on Shigemoto.

Shigemoto realized later that he had acted as a love messenger between Heijū and his mother, and that Heijū had used him. At the time, only his mother's closest attendants and Sanuki would have known. In fact, Sanuki may have sympathized with Heijū; perhaps it was she who suggested that Heijū use the boy to carry messages to and from his mother. Shigemoto could not remember clearly, but he thought that Sanuki had been there when Heijū took him again into the room with the folding screen, to look at his mother's inscription. Not only that: he had the feeling that it was Sanuki who carefully scrubbed his arm, saying as she did so, What a shame it is to wipe this away.

It is unclear whether he had a poem written on his arm only this time, or once or twice again; but when Shigemoto went to the west wing after that, Heijū would be loitering there. Accosting the boy, he would entrust him with a letter. When Shigemoto took it to his mother, she would sometimes write a reply, sometimes not. Gradually she ceased to show the emotion of the first time, and sometimes the expression on her face suggested that she found the letters offensive, until finally Shigemoto felt it an imposition to be employed as Heijū's messenger. Presently Heijū stopped making his appearances, and soon Shigemoto was no longer able to see his mother. His nurse refrained from taking him to his mother's house, and when Shigemoto said he wanted to see his mother, the nurse would say, Your mother is in confinement, because she is going to have a baby soon. Apparently she really was pregnant at the time, but other obstacles seem to have arisen as well to prevent Shigemoto's visits.

Thus Shigemoto had no further opportunities to see his mother. "Mother," to him, was nothing more than the memory of a tearful face that he had glimpsed in his fifth year and the sensory awareness of her fragrant incense. For forty years, memory and awareness were cherished, gradually beautified into an ideal, and purified, until they had become something vastly different from the reality.

Shigemoto's memories of his father are from later than those of his mother. Exactly when they begin is unclear, but probably it was around the time when he could no longer visit his mother. He had hardly ever come in contact with his father before then, and thereafter his father's existence suddenly came into sharp focus. The father he remembered was the very image of a pathetic old man abandoned by his beloved. For that matter, Shigemoto's mother—who did not begrudge a tear for the poem Heijū wrote on his arm—never told him what she thought of his father. When he sat on his mother's lap behind the curtain stands, with her arms around him, he never volunteered anything about his father, nor did his mother ever ask how his father was. Sanuki and the other ladies, too, had little to say about Kunitsune, though they seemed strangely sympathetic to Heijū. The only exception was the nurse, Emon.

9

IT'S NATURAL that you should miss your mother, the nurse said to Shigemoto, but your father is the one who truly deserves our sympathy. He is lonely. You must be a good son and comfort him. Though she did not criticize Shigemoto's mother, she apparently knew about Heijū and disapproved of Sanuki for acting as his intermediary. Her dislike for Sanuki seemed to intensify after she realized that Shigemoto, too, had been used as an intermediary. Might this have led her to discontinue Shigemoto's visits to his mother's house? There's nothing I can do about your going to see your mother, she said to Shigemoto with a frightening glower, but you must not carry messages for anyone.

After Shigemoto's mother had left, his father often

neglected his duties and stayed shut up in his room like an invalid. He looked emaciated and gloomy, even to a casual observer; to his child he was sinister and unapproachable, and Shigemoto was not eager to go to comfort him. His nurse said, Your father is a gentle man. How happy he would be if you went to him. One day she led Shigemoto by the hand to his father's room, slid open the partition, and pushed him inside. His father had always been thin, but now his eyes were sunken and his face shaggy with silver whiskers. He was sitting like a wolf beside his pillow, apparently having just risen from bed. Shigemoto flinched when he felt his father's sharp glance on him; he had been about to say "Father," but the word caught in his throat.

As father and son looked each other over, the fear oppressing Shigemoto's heart gradually abated, to be replaced by an inexpressibly sweet nostalgia. At first he did not recognize its source, but soon he noticed that the room was filled with the fragrance of the incense that his mother had always burned into her robes. Then he saw clothing that his mother used to wear, scattered around his father where he sat—outer robes, unlined robes, narrow-sleeved robes.

Suddenly his father said, "Do you remember this, my boy?" Extending his hard, dry arm like an iron bar, he grasped the collar of a colorful robe.

Shigemoto went to his side. His father held the robe up in front of Shigemoto with both hands, then buried his face in it and remained motionless for a long time. Finally he looked up.

"You must miss your mother too," he said softly, in a tone that invited sympathy. Shigemoto had never looked closely at his father's face before. His eyes were gummy;

most of his front teeth had fallen out; and his voice was hoarse, making it a little hard to understand what he said. Though his tone was intimate, he was neither smiling nor crying. He simply stared into Shigemoto's eyes with an earnest, preoccupied expression that made him look sinister to Shigemoto again.

"Uh-huh." Shigemoto nodded.

His father frowned. "All right, you can go," he said irritably.

Shigemoto did not approach him for some time after that. Your father is at home again today, he would be told, but the news only made him avoid his father's room. His father would stay shut in all day, hardly ever showing himself. Now and then, when he passed the room, Shigemoto would listen at the door for sounds of life inside, but he heard none. He assumed that his father had taken out his mother's robes again and buried himself in their enchanting fragrance.

That year, or perhaps the next, on a crisp, clear autumn afternoon, his father made a rare appearance in the garden and sat absentmindedly on a rock beside the stream. The branches of the bush clover drooped under the weight of their blossoms. Shigemoto had not seen his father for a long time. Resting there on the rock, his father looked like an exhausted traveler, pausing at the roadside in a long journey on foot. His robes were soiled and rumpled, the sleeves and skirts torn and coming apart at the seams. Either there were no longer any serving women to look after him or he refused to let them touch him. Shigemoto saw a radiance on his father's wasted cheeks as the old man's figure caught the red glow of the sun, which had begun to sink toward the west; but he stood five or six steps away, still hesitant to approach. He heard his father mumbling.

Shigemoto could tell that the mumbles were verses his father recited melodiously under his breath. Apparently unaware that Shigemoto was listening beside him, he repeated the same lines two or three times, with his eyes cast down on the surface of the water.

"My boy," he said finally, turning toward the child. "I'll teach you a Chinese poem. It was written by a man named Po Chü-i, of the T'ang. It's probably too difficult for a child to understand, but that doesn't matter. All you have to do is memorize it just as I teach it to you. Then when you're grown up the meaning will come to you.

"Here, sit with me," he said. Shigemoto sat beside his father on the edge of the rock. At first his father spoke slowly, pausing between phrases, so that it would be easy for the child to remember, and waiting for Shigemoto to repeat each phrase before he went on to the next; but as the lesson progressed, he forgot his role as teacher. Giving rein to his emotions, he lifted his voice and began to sing with feeling.

> *Lost, she has turned to snow in the garden;*
> *In flight, she follows the wind above the sea.*
> *In the empyrean she will have found a companion;*
> *Three nights she has not returned to her perch.*
> *Her voice fades beyond the green clouds;*
> *Her form sinks into the brilliant moon.*
> *At the governor's residence hereafter*
> *Who will keep company with this old white head?*

Shigemoto discovered as an adult that the poem was a regulated verse, five words to the line, entitled "Losing My

Crane," from the *Collected Works* of Po Chü-i. At the time, he did not understand what the poem was about, but after that his father sang the lines to himself so often when he was drunk that Shigemoto grew tired of hearing it. He saw in retrospect that his father, likening Shigemoto's departed mother to the crane, had been conveying his anguish through this poem; and even as a child he felt his father's grief communicating itself to him when he heard the sorrowful voice reciting these verses. His voice being hoarse, his father could not produce high notes, nor could he draw his voice out, being short of breath. From a technical point of view, then, his chanting was poor; but when he recited the line "In the empyrean she will have found a companion"; or "Her voice fades beyond the green clouds; Her form sinks into the brilliant moon"; or "Who will keep company with this old white head?" the pathos in his voice transcended technique and could not help but move the listener.

Once Shigemoto had learned to recite the poem, his father said, "Since you were able to memorize that, I'll give you a longer one." The poem he taught Shigemoto next, "Night Rain," was indeed much longer than the first:

There is someone I love,
Far, far away in a distant town.
There is something I feel,
Taking shape deep in my breast.
Though the town is far and I cannot go to it,
There is never a day I do not look up and gaze that way;
Though my feelings are deep and I cannot change them,
There is never a night that I do not ponder,
The more because in the lingering lamplight tonight
I lodge alone in an empty room.

The autumn sky has not yet dawned;
The wind and rain are bleak.
Unless I study the ascetic Dharma,
How shall I forget this heart?

His father often recited the last lines, "Unless I study the ascetic Dharma, How shall I forget this heart?" as if he were speaking to himself, and it may have been under the influence of such lines that he shortly turned to Buddhism. Shigemoto remembered many other lines in fragments, but what poems they come from is unclear: "Late at night I lie down alone; for whom should I dust off the bed?" "Sick, I see my breakfast grow smaller; restless, I know the length of the night." "Gray hairs fall out at dawn, I hate to comb my head; both eyes grow dim in spring, I often use medicine." "Of course I shall empty my wine jar into my stomach; what is to stop me from falling down drunk?" Sometimes his father would recite these lines quietly to himself, standing despondently in a far corner of the garden; at other times he would isolate himself from everyone else, drink saké alone, and weep as he sang them in a passionate voice. Tears would be streaming down his cheeks.

Sanuki was no longer in the household by that time. She must have deserted Shigemoto's father and taken refuge with his mother shortly after she had gone away. As far as Shigemoto could remember, the nurse Emon looked after both Shigemoto and his father. Occasionally she would reprimand his father in the same tone she used on little Shigemoto. She was most severe about his father's drinking.

"Since you have no other pleasures in your old age, it would be all right if you drank just a little, but . . ."

When the nurse spoke to him this way, Shigemoto's father would hang his head dejectedly, like a child who has been scolded by his mother. "I'm sorry I made you worry," he would say meekly. Of course it was inevitable that Shigemoto's father, abandoned in old age by the woman he loved, would turn more than ever to saké, which he had always been fond of, and make it his only companion; but it was also natural for the nurse to worry, because his drunkenness came to exceed all normal bounds. He would apologize obediently when the nurse admonished him, but within the day he would be falling-down drunk again. He could be forgiven for reciting Chinese poems and wailing aloud, but often he would wander away in the middle of the night and not return for two or three days.

"Where could he have gone?" the nurse and the serving women would sigh as they put their heads together. It was not unusual for them to send someone inconspicuously to search for him. Shigemoto was distressed as well. After two or three days his father would suddenly turn up at the door, or he would come back to his room unnoticed and go to bed, or someone would find him and bring him home. Once, the searchers found him lying in a remote field far from the capital. When he arrived at the house he looked like a mendicant priest, his hair disheveled, his robes torn, his arms and legs smeared with mud. The nurse was so astonished she could only cry, "Oh!" and dissolve into tears. Shigemoto's father looked down sheepishly. He slipped away to his room without a word and buried his face in the bedding.

"At this rate he really will go mad, or else hurt himself," the nurse was always saying behind his back. Then, abruptly, he gave up the saké he had loved so much.

Shigemoto does not explain what led his father to give

up saké. He was first aware of the change when his nurse said to him, "How admirable your father has become. He spends the whole day quietly reading the sūtras." Probably his father had tried to drown the longing for his mother with saké and then, realizing that saké was ineffective, turned for help to the Buddha's compassion. In other words, he followed the suggestion of Po Chü-i's poem: "Unless I study the ascetic Dharma, How shall I forget this heart?" It would have been around a year before his death, when Shigemoto was in about his seventh year. His father's wildness was gone by then: he would often spend the entire day in his chapel, meditating, reading sūtras, or listening to a virtuous monk whom he had invited to discourse on the Dharma. The nurse and the serving women breathed easier. The master has settled down, they said happily; now we needn't worry. To Shigemoto, though, his father was as sinister and unapproachable as ever.

When the chapel was too quiet, the nurse would say, "Young master, go take a peek at your father and see what he's doing." Shigemoto would approach the chapel fearfully, kneel at the threshold, put his hand silently to the partition, and slide it open an inch. A painting of the bodhisattva Samantabhadra hung on the wall directly opposite; facing it was his father, seated stiffly and perfectly still. Shigemoto could see only his father's back. Though he watched for some time, his father neither recited a sūtra, looked at a book, nor burned incense; he just sat in silence.

"What is Father doing?" Shigemoto asked his nurse.

"He's practicing what is called the Contemplation of Impurity," she replied.

Since the Contemplation of Impurity involves an exceedingly difficult theory, the nurse was not able to give a

full explanation. In brief, a person who practices the Contemplation of Impurity will come to understand that the
various carnal pleasures of mankind are nothing more than
momentary illusions, whereupon he will no longer find his
beloved lovable; and he will know that things beautiful to
behold, delicious to eat, or pleasing to smell are in fact not
beautiful, delicious, or pleasing, but are filthy things. Your
father is practicing this discipline, the nurse said, because
he is trying to get over the loss of your mother.

In this connection, Shigemoto had a terrifying memory
of his father, one that he could never forget. It happened
around this time. His father would sit quietly meditating
around the clock for days at a time. Overcome with curiosity about when he ate and slept, Shigemoto crept from his
bedroom late one night, taking care that his nurse did not
notice, and went to the chapel. A light was burning faintly
beyond the partition, and his father was seated in the same
position as he had assumed during the day. However long
Shigemoto peered through the opening, his father remained immobile as a statue. Shigemoto quietly shut the
partition, returned to his room, and went to bed. Troubled
the next night too, he went again to look and found his
father exactly as he had been the night before. Again on the
third night, driven by curiosity, Shigemoto tiptoed to the
chapel, opened the partition an inch, and held his breath.
The flame on the lamp stand flickered, though there was no
draft. Just then his father's shoulders swayed and his body
stirred. The movements were so sluggish that Shigemoto
could not guess their purpose at first, but presently his
father placed one hand on the floor and, taking a deep
breath as though he were lifting a heavy object, slowly
pulled himself up to a standing position. His age would

have made him rise slowly in any case; since he had been sitting in a formal position for so long, he could not have stood up otherwise. Once on his feet, he staggered out of the room.

Surprised and curious, Shigemoto followed him. His father peered straight ahead as he went down the steps, put on a pair of sturdy straw sandals, and stood on the ground. The moon shone a clear white, and the insects were singing—the season was autumn, without question; but when Shigemoto stepped into the garden after him and slipped on a pair of adult sandals, he thought it might be winter, because the soles of his feet were so cold he felt as if he were wading through ice water, and the ground was white in the moonlight, as if it were covered with frost. His father's shadow, sharply defined on the ground, swayed as he walked. Shigemoto took care not to step on it as he followed at a distance. He might have been discovered had his father looked back, but his father seemed to be deep in meditation as he walked. Passing through the gate, he quickened his pace as though he had a clear objective in mind.

A man of eighty and a child of six or seven could not have walked very far, but it felt like a long way to Shigemoto. Though he trailed far behind his father, he had no fear of losing him, because no one else was on the road this late at night, and his father's distant figure reflected the white glow of the moon. At first the road took them past rows of mansions, each one enclosed behind imposing earthen walls. These gradually gave way to shabby wicker fences and wretched houses whose low, shingled roofs were weighted down by stones. Then these thinned out, to be replaced by puddles and open land covered with tall plumed grasses. The insect chorus would stop abruptly as the humans approached a clump of grass, and resume when they had passed, steadily more clamorous and insistent, like rain, toward the outskirts of the city. Presently there were no houses at all, only luxuriant grasses as far as he could see and, winding through it, a narrow path. Though the path had no forks, it twisted this way and that way through grasses growing taller than a man. Shigemoto sometimes lost sight of his father now; he moved up to within a few yards. As he pushed his way through the grasses that arched over the path from both sides, his sleeves and skirts became soaked with dew and cold drops ran down the back of his neck.

Coming to a stream spanned by a bridge, his father crossed and, instead of taking the path straight ahead, descended to the water's edge and walked downstream along a narrow, sandy bank. About one hundred yards down from the bridge were three or four burial mounds, constructed on a low, flat rise. The earth in them was soft and fresh, and the wooden markers erected on top of each mound were still white, their inscriptions clearly legible in the moonlight. Some graves had been planted with small pines or cedars instead of wooden markers; others, not in the form of a mound, had been enclosed by a fence and marked with a heap of rocks and a five-tier stone monument. In the simplest graves, the body was covered with nothing more than a woven mat and an offering of flowers. A few of the markers had fallen in a recent typhoon, and soil had been washed away from some of the mounds, partially exposing the bodies that lay beneath.

Shigemoto's father wandered among the mounds as though he were looking for something, and Shigemoto was right on his heels; whether his father was conscious of being followed or not, he had not once looked back. A dog that had been gorging itself on corpses sprang from a clump of grass and ran away in a panic, but Shigemoto's father paid no attention. He was extraordinarily tense and focused— Shigemoto could see this even from behind. Before long his father came to a halt, and Shigemoto stopped in his tracks. At that instant he saw a sight that made his hair stand on end.

Moonlight, like a blanket of snow, paints out everything uniformly in a phosphoric color, and in the first moment Shigemoto could not quite distinguish the strange shape lying on the ground before him; but looking hard, he realized that it was the rotting corpse of a young woman. He could tell from the flesh remaining on her limbs and from the tone of the skin that it was a young woman; but her long hair, skin and all, had fallen from the skull like a wig, her face had become a lump of shapeless flesh, viscera spilled from her abdomen, and the entire body was wriggling with maggots. It is not difficult to imagine the horror of seeing such a thing in moonlight as bright as the day. Shigemoto stood as if lashed to the sight, unable to avert his face in fear, to move his body, or, much less, to cry out. His father calmly approached the corpse, bowed to it reverently, and knelt beside it on a straw mat. Sitting upright and motionless as he had in the chapel, he began to meditate, now looking at the corpse, now half closing his eyes.

The moon came out even more brightly, as if it had been polished, and deepened the desolation around them. Aside from the rustle of the tall grasses in an occasional breeze, the only sound was the dinning of the insects. The sight of his father kneeling like a solitary shadow in these surroundings made Shigemoto feel that he had been drawn into a weird dream world, but he was summoned back willy-nilly to the world of reality by the putrid smell that assaulted his nostrils.

Just where it was that Shigemoto's father saw the woman's corpse is not clear. There must have been many spots where corpses were abandoned in the Kyoto of the time. When many victims died in epidemics of smallpox or measles, fear of contagion and a lack of proper facilities forced people to carry the bodies to the nearest open land and bury them with no more than a token covering of earth or a straw mat. This must have been such a place.

10

WHILE his father meditated on the corpse, Shigemoto crouched behind one of the mounds and held his breath. The moon had been directly overhead; when it had sunk toward the west, casting long shadows across the ground from the cluster of wooden grave markers behind which Shigemoto was hiding, his father finally rose and started for home. Shigemoto followed him along the path on which they had come. Just after recrossing the bridge and entering the field of tall plumed grasses, his father addressed him unexpectedly.

"My boy . . . my boy, what do you think I was doing there tonight?" Stopping on the path and looking back, he waited for Shigemoto to catch up with him.

"I knew that you were following me. I had something on my mind and let you do as you wanted. . . ."

Shigemoto still said nothing, and so his father continued, in a gentler, more intimate tone. "I'm not going to scold you, my boy. Tell me the truth. You were watching me from the beginning tonight, weren't you?"

Shigemoto nodded. "I was worried about you," he said by way of explanation.

"You thought I'd gone mad, didn't you?" He looked amused and seemed to laugh weakly, but his laugh was too faint to hear. "You're not the only one. Everyone seems to think so. . . . But I'm not crazy. There's a reason for what I'm doing. I'll tell you the reason if it will reassure you. . . . What do you say? Will you listen?"

This is what Shigemoto's father told him as they walked together back to the house. At the time, of course, Shigemoto could not possibly grasp even the gist of what his father said; and what he recorded in his diary was not his father's words, just as he spoke them, but Shigemoto's own interpretations as an adult many years later. It has to do with what Buddhists call the Contemplation of Impurity. Being ignorant of Buddhist doctrine, I doubt whether I can describe it accurately. I have consulted a scholar of the Tendai sect, who has shown me many kindnesses over the years, and have borrowed some reference books from him; but the more one looks into the subject, the more esoteric and obscure it becomes. There is no need to explain the concept in depth here, however, and so, to keep matters in order, I will touch only on the aspects that are necessary for the progress of this tale.

One book I know of that deals with the Contemplation of Impurity in simple language (and there are probably others) is called *Companion for a Quiet Life,* attributed by some to the monk Jichin, by others to the priest Shōgatsubō Keisei.* It is a selection of spiritual biographies and stories about famous priests and wise men that had been omitted from *A Collection of Religious Awakenings†* and other compilations. It includes, in the first volume, "How a Lowly Monk Devoted Himself to the Contemplation of Impurity in His Spare Time," "How a Lowly Man's Heart Was Awakened by His Seeing a Corpse in a Field," and "About a Woman's Corpse on the Karahashi Riverbed"; and in the second volume, "About Seeing the Impure Form of a Royal Lady-in-Waiting." Reading these gives one a general understanding of the Contemplation of Impurity.

As an example, here is a story from *Companion for a Quiet Life.*

Long ago there was a young monk named Chūgen, in the service of a virtuous sage on Mount Hiei. Though a monk, he was more like a sexton, serving the sage in various capacities, and because he always served his master dutifully, carried out every command without fail, and had a truly faithful nature, the sage placed no little confidence in him. After a time, this youth began to disappear every evening and return early the next morning. Suspecting that he was visiting the town of Sakamoto every night, the sage was secretly furious. When the monk came back in the morning he would be downcast, reluctant to face anyone, and always on the point of tears. Everyone from the sage

---

Kankyo no tomo, a collection of Buddhist tales compiled in 1222. Jichin is better known as Jien, 1155–1225. Keisei lived 1189–1268.
†*Hosshinshū,* thirteenth century.

on down concluded that things were not going well with
the woman the young monk was visiting; yes, that had to
be it. One night the sage sent a servant to follow him. The
youth descended the mountain through Nishi-Sakamoto
(not Sakamoto in the province of Ōmi, but the western foot
of Mount Hiei, in the neighborhood that is now called
Ichijōji, Sakyō Ward, Kyoto) to Rendai Moor. Puzzled, the
servant watched closely to see what he was doing. Tramp-
ing his way here and there through the grasses, the monk
approached an unspeakably rotten corpse and began to
pray, with his eyes sometimes closed, sometimes open. He
cried aloud as he repeated his prayers again and again. This
continued all night until, hearing the bells at dawn, he
dried his tears and returned to the temple. The servant, too,
was deeply moved and wept on his way back. What happened? the sage asked his servant. It is no wonder that he
has been so depressed, the servant replied, describing what
he had seen. . . . And that is why he disappears every
evening, he concluded. It was a grave sin for us to doubt
him without good reason, a man who practices the austerities of a saint. The sage was astonished. After that he
revered the monk Chūgen and no longer treated him as an
ordinary person. One morning Chūgen made rice gruel
and served it for breakfast. Assuring himself that no one
else was around, the sage asked him, Are the rumors true,
that you are practicing the Contemplation of Impurity?
Not at all, the monk said. That is for great men of learning
to do. You can tell by looking at me whether I am capable
of it. The sage persisted. Everyone knows about you now,
he said. For some time I, too, have thought of you as a man
to revere. Keep nothing from me. In that case, said Chūgen,
I shall speak. Truly, I have no deep knowledge of anything,

but I understand a little. Your austerities must have some effect, said the sage. Try meditating on this gruel. The youth picked up the tray, covered the gruel, and meditated for a time with his eyes closed. When he removed the lid, the gruel had turned into white worms. The sage wept copiously. You must be my teacher, he said, pressing his hands together.

Such is the story of "How a Lowly Monk Devoted Himself to the Contemplation of Impurity in His Spare Time." "It was truly a marvelous thing," says the author of *Companion for a Quiet Life*. He adds this commentary: The Great T'ien-t'ai Master* explains in *First Steps in Meditation*† that even an ignorant man will be more successful in meditation if he goes to a burial mound and looks at a decomposing corpse. The monk Chūgen must have learned this. In *The Great Cessation and Insight*,‡ the Master explains Insight this way: "Mountains and rivers are all impure. Food and clothing, too, are impure. Rice is like white worms; robes are like the skins of stinking things." The monk Chūgen's meditation spontaneously coincided with these holy teachings. A Buddhist *bhiksu* of India, too, taught that vessels are like skulls, rice like worms, and clothing like the skins of serpents; and the Chinese Master of Discipline Tao-hsüan,** too, taught that vessels are human bones, rice is human flesh. How wonderful it is that an unlearned monk who could not have known the teachings of these masters should put them into practice. Even

---

*Chih-i (538–597).
†*Tz'u-ti Ch'an-mên*, sixth century.
‡*Mo-ho Chih-kuan*, 594.
**Tao-hsüan lived 596–667.

if one is unable to achieve the stage reached by the monk Chūgen, the Five Passions will gradually fade away and one's outlook will change when one has begun to understand this principle. "Those who do not grasp this truth are greedy for delicate food and indignant over coarse food and worn clothing. Though good and bad may change, both alike are seeds of the cycle of rebirth. . . . But how profitless they are, these ephemeral things seen in a dream; and for them we suffer through the long sleep of illusion. These are matters that we must ponder."

"How a Lowly Man's Heart Was Awakened by His Seeing a Corpse in a Field" carries a moral of roughly the same purport. The gist of the story is that a man sees the wretched corpse of a woman in a field and cannot shake the memory of her features, even after he has returned home. Lying with his wife at night, he runs his hands over her face: her forehead, nose, and lips all seem to him identical to the dead woman's features, and he awakens to the truth of Impermanence. *Cessation and Insight* explains everything from dying and decomposition to gathering the bones and burning them. Seeing such things is truly heartbreaking. For a man ignorant of these texts to awaken on his own," says the author, is all the more marvelous.

To cultivate this understanding, one sits quietly alone like a Zen monk doing *zazen* and meditates, eyes closed, with the mind focused on one thing. That thing can be, for example, contemplation of the fact that each of us is a product of our parents' carnal pleasure and is born of impure, unclean fluids. In the words of the *Commentary on the Great Wisdom Sūtra*, "The body's worms of desire: when people copulate, the male worm, a white essence, comes forth like tears, and the female worm, a red essence, comes forth like vomit; bone-marrow oil flows and discharges these two worms like vomit and tears," and the fusion of these two drops, red and white, is our flesh. Next, one considers the facts that at birth we emerge from a filthy passageway; and that after we are born we eliminate feces and urine, dribble mucus from our noses, expel foul breath from our mouths, and excrete slimy perspiration from our armpits; and that our bodies brim with feces, urine, pus, blood, and fat, and that our entrails are full of filth and all sorts of worms; and that after we die, animals eat our corpses and birds peck at us, our limbs come off and are carried away, our raw stench assaults the noses of people miles away, our skin turns reddish black, and our corpses are more hideous than a dog's. In short, one contemplates the fact that our bodies are at all times impure, even before birth and after death.

The Great Cessation and Insight explains the subject in great detail. It gives, for example, the proper order of these meditations and identifies "the Impurity of the Seed," or "the Impurity of the Five Seeds," as the reason for the impurity of the human body. It also depicts exhaustively the stages of change in a human corpse, explaining that the first stage is the Putrefaction Phase; second, the Gore Phase; third, the Suppuration Phase; fourth, the Discoloration Phase; and fifth, the Omophagous Phase. As long as one does not perceive these phases clearly, he will fall recklessly in love and attach himself to others; but if he sees them with perfect clarity, all desiring will cease, and things that until a moment before he had considered beautiful will be repulsive to him. It is, says the text, like being able to eat as long as one is not looking at feces, but after inhaling their stench one feels sick and can eat no longer.

Nevertheless, it sometimes happens that one cannot master the Contemplation of Impurity by sitting quietly, thinking about these truths, and picturing the stages of change. Another technique is to go where bodies are discarded and watch with one's own eyes as the phenomena described in *Cessation and Insight* occur. This is what the monk Chūgen did. And if one views the transformations of the corpses not once or twice but repeatedly—like our monk, who made his way down the mountain to Rendai Moor every night—and accustoms one's eyes to the Putrefaction Phase, the Gore Phase, the Suppuration Phase, and so on, then finally he will be able to see them vividly just by sitting erect in a room with his eyes closed. Not only that: it even happens that a woman who strikes everyone else as a paragon of beauty will appear to the ascetic as a lump of odious, putrid flesh, or as a mass of blood and pus. Sometimes an ascetic will test the success of his training by fetching a beautiful woman and positioning himself before her to meditate. And when an ascetic who has achieved many such successes practices the Contemplation of Impurity, a living beauty will come to look revolting, not only in the subjective view of the ascetic himself, but in the eyes of onlookers as well. This is the significance of the gruel that changed into a clump of white worms when Chūgen meditated at his master's command. One who has mastered the Contemplation of Impurity can actually perform marvels of this kind.

Now, according to Captain Shigemoto's diary, Shigemoto's father tried to practice the Contemplation of Impurity. It is clear that the old Major Counselor, unable to bear his sorrow any longer, turned to Buddhism in an attempt to conquer the phantom of that lost crane—the beautiful lady whose voice had faded beyond the green clouds, whose splendid image, sinking into the brilliant moon, still clung to his eyes. Shigemoto's father began that night with an explanation of the Contemplation of Impurity and told Shigemoto that he wanted somehow to forget his bitterness and longing for the one who had abandoned him, to erase her lovely image from the depths of his heart, and to sever himself from earthly passions. His actions might look insane to others, but he was now engaged in this ascetic discipline.

"Then tonight isn't the first time you've gone to look at things like that?" Shigemoto asked during a pause in his father's long narration. His father nodded emphatically. For some months now he had chosen bright, moonlit nights, waited until everyone else in the house was asleep, and slipped out to burial places in distant fields, where he would meditate until daybreak, then return home quietly.

"And are you enlightened now, Father?" Shigemoto asked.

"No." His father stopped. Looking toward the moon on the crest of the distant mountains, he sighed. "Far from it. Mastering the Contemplation of Impurity isn't as easy as it sounds."

After that, his father did not respond when Shigemoto spoke to him; he seemed preoccupied and hardly said a word, all the way back to the house.

That night was the only time Shigemoto accompanied his father on one of his nocturnal walks. Since his father had slipped out in the same way several times before, he undoubtedly wandered out after that as well. Late the next night, for example, Shigemoto heard his father softly open the door and go out; but his father did not invite Shigemoto to go along, nor did Shigemoto want to follow him again.

In later years Shigemoto sometimes wondered why his father had confided that night in a young, naive child. It was the only time in his life that he had such a long conversation with his father. Indeed, his father had done all the talking, and Shigemoto had been his audience. His father's tone had been solemn at first and had a touch of melancholy that awed the little boy; but as he continued to speak, he seemed to be pleading with his son, and finally—or perhaps it was Shigemoto's imagination—the voice sounded tearful. In his child's heart, Shigemoto feared that his father—so agitated that he forgot he was talking to a small child—could never succeed in meditation, that all his devotions would prove to be wasted effort. He could sympathize with the process that had led his father, in agony day and night as he pursued the image of his beloved, to seek release from his suffering in the Way of the Buddha, and he felt both pity and empathy for him. But in truth he could not repress a certain antagonism, something like indignation, against his father for likening his mother to an odious roadside corpse, for thinking of her as a revolting, rotted thing, instead of striving to cherish her beautiful image just as it was. Several times, listening to his father, Shigemoto wanted to call out, "Father, please don't make Mother into something dirty." He had barely been able to restrain himself from doing so.

Shigemoto's father died about ten months later, at summer's end in the following year. Was he able to gain release from the world of sexual passion by the time of his death? Could he view as a worthless lump of putrid flesh the woman he had pined for, and die purely, nobly, free from illusion and doubt? Or did he die as the boy supposed, undelivered by the Buddha, tormented again by the phantom of his beloved, his eighty-year-old breast still ablaze with passion? . . . Shigemoto is unable to offer any conclusive evidence one way or the other on the outcome of his father's inner struggle; but from the fact that his father's death was not an easy passing, such as others might envy, he concluded that his supposition had not been mistaken.

Ordinary human nature suggests that a man unable to forget his runaway wife might treat the son she had borne him with a little more affection, that transferring his love from his wife to his child would ease his suffering; but this was not the case with Shigemoto's father. If he could not bring back the wife who had abandoned him, he certainly would not be placated or distracted by anyone else—not even by his own son, in whose veins her blood flowed. That is how pure and single-minded was his father's love for his mother. Shigemoto was not entirely without memories of his father speaking to him gently, but the topic had always been his mother; at other times his father had been indifferent toward him. When Shigemoto considered that his father was so preoccupied with his mother that he had no time for his child, he did not resent the indifference; on the contrary, he was happy that his father felt that way. In any case, his father grew more and more indifferent to his child after that night and appeared not to give him a thought. He was like a man staring at a point of nothingness before his eyes. That being the case, Shigemoto heard nothing about his father's inner life during that last year; but he noticed that his father had once again developed a taste for the saké he had given up for some time; though his father still shut himself up in his chapel, the painting of the bodhisattva Samantabhadra no longer hung on the wall; and he began again to recite poems by Po Chü-i instead of sūtras.

ONE WISHES for even a little more detailed information about the old Counselor's state of mind at the time of his death, but since nothing further is to be found in Shigemoto's chronicle, we can only judge from the circumstances and conclude that he died unredeemed—defeated by the beautiful phantasm of his beloved and clinging to Eternal Illusion. This would have been a sad end for the old Counselor himself, but we can assume that it was the happiest possible outcome from Shigemoto's point of view, since it means that his father died without desecrating his mother's beauty.

The year after the old Counselor's death, Minister of the Left Shihei died, and over the next forty years his line faded out, as we have seen. The throne passed from Emperors Daigo and Suzaku to Murakami, and society went through various shifts and changes, including the vicissitudes of the Fujiwara and Sugawara clans. Shigemoto grew up during these years and reached the rank of Lesser Captain, but his diary, preoccupied with his mother, neglects his own affairs. It does give the impression that he was taken in and reared by his nurse for some years after his father's death. As for the old woman Sanuki, we know that she followed her mistress and became an attendant at Hon'in, but she does not appear in the diary again. Nor is there any mention of the half-brothers with whom Shigemoto shared a father, or of their mothers; perhaps

Shigemoto had no dealings with them. For his younger half-brother Atsutada, however—with whom he shared the same mother—Shigemoto secretly felt the greatest affection. Shigemoto and Atsutada differed in rank and family status, and the trouble between their fathers over the lady stood between them. Apparently there was reserve on both sides and each avoided intimacy with the other, but Shigemoto was nevertheless well disposed toward Atsutada and, watching his activities with interest, prayed from a distance for his good fortune. In the last analysis, this was because Atsutada looked like his mother: the sight of the Middle Counselor filled Shigemoto with an almost unbearable nostalgia, he writes several times, because it reminded him of his mother's appearance when he had met her many years before. It also grieved him that he himself resembled his father, and not his mother; this, he says, is probably why his father longed only for his mother after she ran away and paid no attention to him. He envied Atsutada for living with his mother, even after Shihei's death, and assumed that she loved the handsome Atsutada but could never be fond of an ugly son like Shigemoto, even if he had been able to live with her. Just as she disliked his father, he says, she must dislike him as well.

And how did the object of Shigemoto's intense longing, his mother, the Ariwara lady, live out her years? She must have been twenty-four or -five when Shihei predeceased her; did she live quietly after that as a beautiful young widow? or did she become involved with a third man, and a fourth? Since she had had Heijū as a lover while she was still married to the old Counselor, it would not be surprising if she had at least exchanged sweet whispers with someone discreetly, but nothing is known today about such

matters. Shigemoto, who loved his mother even more single-mindedly than his father had, would scarcely have
recorded unsavory rumors about his mother in any case;
but let us accept his diary for now and assume that his
mother lived out her days as a lonely, modest widow,
watching with pleasure as Atsutada, the orphan of the
Minister of the Left, grew up. What must her thoughts have
been, on the other hand, when she learned that her former
husband, the old Counselor, had died in an agony of longing for her, or that Heijū, out of vexation at being rejected
by her, had chased Jijū and lost his life as a result? While
the Minister of the Left still wielded his authority she
would have been an object of envy, esteemed by many as
the Lady of Hon'in, but after the Minister's death the
flowering fortunes of former times would have faded like a
dream in the morning, leaving her to lament that nothing
turned out any longer as she wished. The men died off who
had felt such dreadful passion for her, the relatives of the
Minister of the Left fell one by one under the curse of the
Sugawara Minister, and her beloved son Atsutada was
taken by death—seeing these things, she must have felt the
piercing winds of Impermanence.

But why did Shigemoto make no attempt to approach
his mother, when he longed for her so much? Whatever
might have been the case while the Minister of the Left was
still alive, there would seem to have been no obstacle to
meeting her after the Minister's death; but if it is true that
Shigemoto avoided even Atsutada, then a man of his rank
would have had to refrain all the more from visiting his
mother. Shigemoto's diary has this to say on the subject:
Several times when he was ten or eleven years old he did
express a wish to meet his mother, but his nurse admon-

ished him each time: Society is not so simple as that; your mother belongs to a different family now. She is no longer your mother. She is the mother of someone much higher in rank than we are. . . . Shigemoto also says that, reaching maturity, he left his nurse and became independent; and arriving at an age where he could make decisions for himself, he understood better and better the truth of what his nurse had told him and could not easily find a chance to meet his mother. He felt the distance between himself and his mother increase with each passing year. Though her husband the Minister of the Left was dead, Shigemoto still imagined his mother as a person far beyond his reach above the clouds, the widow of a noble house, attended by servants and spending her days behind the jeweled curtains of a splendid mansion. It was after all as his nurse had said: the lady was no longer someone that a man like him could call "mother." Sadly, he would have to think of "mother" as no longer being of this world. In any case, Shigemoto seems to have been overly sensitive about his mother, believing as he did that she had deserted him along with his father, and such feelings might well have increased the psychological distance between him and his mother.

Meanwhile Atsutada died in the third month of 943, and before long his mother took Buddhist vows. Shigemoto would of course have heard the news. Presumably Atsutada had been one of the barriers that stood between Shigemoto and his mother, and now that Atsutada was gone, Shigemoto fortuitously had his chance and could easily have found a way to meet his mother if he had so desired. The proprieties and regulations of the floating world that had impeded his way before had now been completely removed, and what is more, Shigemoto had also undoubtedly heard that his mother was living as a nun in a hut near Atsutada's villa at Nishi-Sakamoto. She was no longer surrounded by guards; the brushwood gate before her grass hut would turn away no one who approached but would be open to all. Shigemoto must have been tempted, but there are indications that he hesitated for a time, still unable to make up his mind. Shyness and oversensitivity would have been partly to blame; but perhaps Shigemoto had yet another reason to fear a meeting with his real mother.

It seems likely that Shigemoto wanted to go on forever adoring his mother just as he had seen her in his childhood. He had been angry with his father, deploring the desecration of his mother's image when the old Counselor practiced the Contemplation of Impurity, and during forty years of separation he had cherished an idealized version of his mother, which he had constructed from the image that lingered vaguely in his memory. What would she look like now, forty years later, having left the world after so many changes and become a servant of the Buddha? The mother Shigemoto remembered was an aristocratic woman of twenty or twenty-one, with long hair and full cheeks, but his mother the nun, living alone in a hut at Nishi-Sakamoto, was an old woman past sixty years of age. The thought must naturally have caused Shigemoto to shrink from facing cold reality. It may have seemed far better to embrace forever the image of the past, savoring his memories of her gentle voice, the sweet fragrance of her incense, and the sensation of her brush caressing his arm, rather than to drink rashly from the cup of disillusionment. Shigemoto does not confess as much, but one supposes that something of the sort lay behind the years that passed fruitlessly, even after his mother had become a nun.

That Atsutada had a villa in Nishi-Sakamoto (the present Ichijōji, Sakyō Ward, Kyoto), the district where Shigemoto's mother lived after taking Buddhist vows, is clear from a poem by Ise in Book 8 of the *Collection of Gleanings*:

Written on a boulder by a waterfall at Provisional Middle Counselor Atsutada's mountain villa at Nishi-Sakamoto:

*In the cascade he sends down, drawing from the
    quiet Otowa,
The heart of the man is revealed.*

The villa would not have been far by horse from the center of Kyoto. In those days Shigemoto often called on Jōshinbō Ryōgen at Yokawa on Mount Hiei for instruction in Buddhism. If he had taken Kirara Slope down the mountain on his way home, he would have emerged at the village where his mother lived. Indeed, sometimes he would gaze out lovingly from the top of the mountain at the sky over Nishi-Sakamoto, and at times his feet would turn spontaneously in that direction; but he would always check himself and choose a different route.

Then in the spring some years later, Shigemoto spent a night at Ryōgen's cell in Yokawa. Leaving the cottage early in the afternoon of the next day, he passed the Western Precinct and the Lecture Hall and arrived at the crossroads by the Komponchūdō, where, feeling a sudden tugging at his heart, he took the path toward Kirara Slope. "Sudden" does not mean that the idea had come to him abruptly: he had wanted to take this path for some time, and something had always stopped him from carrying out his wish; but now, on this spring day in the middle of the Third Month, enticed by the view of the distant mountains shrouded in mist and by the clouds of cherry blossoms in the valleys here and there, he thought he would like to take a stroll. Also, though he had no other objective in mind, he thought he would like to see the village where his mother lived, since this route would take him to Nishi-Sakamoto.

The sun was inclining toward the west as Shigemoto started down the slope, and a luscious, hazy moon glowed in the sky by the time he passed the Jizō Hall at Mizunomi Pass and arrived at the foot of the mountain, where Otowa Falls echoed in his ears. Mibu no Tadamine's poem is said to be about this waterfall:

> *The waters above this foaming fall have piled up*
> *the years*
> *And seem to have aged—there is not a single*
> *black strand.*

At its base, the waterfall becomes a narrow stream called the Otowa River, and the path descends along the river-bank. Following it casually, Shigemoto came to a low, rough-woven fence, beyond which he could see through the garden trees to a house that looked like a villa. Stepping over the fence where it had rotted and collapsed, he took two or three steps into the enclosure and examined the surroundings. Everything was perfectly still; there were no signs that anyone lived here. Situated between the peaks of Mount Hiei, towering to the east, and a gentle downward slope toward the west, the garden must have been splendid in its time, with its pond, ornamental stones, artificial hill, and stream; but now it was a shambles, weeds covering the ground and creepers clinging to the tree trunks.

Being heavily wooded and near the mountains, the area seemed far from the sun, and especially now, at twilight, Shigemoto felt a chill in the air. Pushing his way through piles of last year's fallen leaves, he approached what appeared to be the main hall. It seemed to be abandoned: the shutters were firmly bolted, and though dusk had come, no light escaped from inside. While he sat on the front steps to rest, Shigemoto noticed that one of the doors was loose, its hinges having worn out. Stepping up to floor level, he peered inside, but the interior was dark and gave off a damp, moldy smell. As he considered whose residence this might have been, Shigemoto realized that it could well be the late Middle Counselor's villa. Perhaps there was no one to live in it after the Counselor's death, and it had been left to go to ruin. If so, his mother, who had lived with the Middle Counselor in this villa and occupied a hut nearby after his death, would probably not be living on this site anymore. No woman, even one who had abandoned the world, could live in such a lonely spot. . . . Pursuing these thoughts, Shigemoto rested for a while, conscious of the intense quiet. The growing darkness and desolation pressed in on him from all sides, but the realization that his mother might once have lived here kept him from moving on right away.

Then he heard the murmur of a brook, mingled with the cries of an owl. Rising, he followed the sound along the garden stream, around the pond, over the artificial hill, and through the shrubbery to a waterfall. Seven or eight feet in height, the cliff was not steep but was a gentle incline on which interestingly shaped rocks had been placed, so that the falling water twisted and foamed between them. From atop the cliff, maples and pines spread their interlacing branches over the falls. No doubt the water had been diverted here from the Otowa River, which Shigemoto had been following shortly before. Ise's poem came to him: "The cascade he sends down, drawing from the quiet Otowa." Yes, it was clear to Shigemoto now that the "cascade" of the poem was this stream, and he could no longer doubt that the villa had been that of the late Middle Counselor.

As the color of twilight deepened further, Shigemoto could barely distinguish the surface of the water from the surrounding darkness; he thought of leaving but was still reluctant. Stepping from rock to rock, he ascended the rapids and climbed beyond the mouth of the waterfall. Here he seemed to be outside the enclosure, for the landscape, gradually reverting to an ordinary hillside, did not have the look of a man-made garden; but then, on a bluff above the stream, he saw a large cherry tree blossoming so radiantly that it seemed to fling back the evening darkness that floated about it. Tsurayuki's poem "Scattered deep in the hills with none to see them" refers to autumn leaves, but at a time like this in a glen like this one, a cherry tree reveling unseen in the spring was no less of a "brocade worn by night."* Rooted a little above the path, the tree towered in isolation and spread its branches like an umbrella, casting a bewitching pale glow over the surroundings. As many know from experience, it is more unnerving to encounter a beautiful young woman walking alone at night on a dark, lonely road than to meet a man in the same

---

*Ki no Tsurayuki, *Kokinshū* 297, "Composed when he went to the northern hills to look at the foliage":

> *Scattered deep in the hills with none to see them,*
> *These tinted leaves are brocades worn by night.*

circumstances. This evening cherry, too, blossoming quietly in isolation, seemed to be shadowed by a demonic
beauty. Doubting his eyes, Shigemoto did not approach the
tree directly but gazed at it from a distance. The bluff on
which the cherry grew consisted almost entirely of one
huge, mossy boulder, rising about ten feet above the surface of the water. A rivulet of water sprang from somewhere, trickled down the bluff, and fell into the stream;
halfway down the bluff, the blossoms of a clump of kerria
snuggled up to the water. It was odd—the hour had grown
late, and yet from where he stood, Shigemoto could make
out vividly the details of the scene. At first he thought that
the cherry blossoms might function like snow to lift objects
out of the surrounding darkness; but it was not a light from
the blossoms—just now the moon in the sky above them
had grown brighter. The ground was damp and the air cold
against his skin; but the sky was lightly overcast, as one
expects in the Third Month, and the hazy moon shone
through the cloud of blossoms, so that the corner of the
glen where the evening cherry cast its faint glow was
caught in a phantasmic beam of light.

As a child, Shigemoto had followed his father along a
narrow path through the fields and witnessed a ghastly
scene under the white glow of the moon; but it had been
the sharp, clear moon of autumn midnight, not the dim
moon of tonight, soft and warm like silk floss. The moon
that night had illuminated even the tiniest objects on the
ground and clearly distinguished each maggot that wrig-
gled in the corpse's entrails; but the moon tonight, while
showing things as they were—the threadlike trickle of
spring water, the cherry petals fluttering in ones and twos
through the motionless air to the ground, the yellow of the

kerria blossoms—framed them all with a fuzzy line like pictures in a magic lantern, giving the impression of a surreal world sketched for a moment in the air, like a mirage that would vanish with a blink of the eye. . . .

Because of this strange, distinctive light, Shigemoto was uncertain how long it had been there when he saw something totally unexpected: a white, fluffy object swaying under the cherry tree. A blossom-laden branch drooped over it, and Shigemoto had not distinguished between them at first; but the white, fluffy object—too large to be a clump of blossoms—might have been fluttering there for some time before he noticed it. In fact, Shigemoto recognized almost immediately that it must be a diminutive monk—or more likely a nun, judging from the short stature and the narrow shoulders—standing by the trunk of the cherry tree, and that what he had seen swaying in the breeze was the cloth that covered the nun's head, a white silk hood of the kind that elderly monks and nuns often use to ward off the cold. But the moment he recognized this, he thought: No, it is a dream. What would a nun be doing in such a place? Either I am dreaming, or the fairy of that demonic evening cherry has shown itself. . . . Something in him wanted to deny the world of his senses, and he tried not to believe what he saw clearly with his eyes.

Try as he might to deny it, however, the human figure grew more distinct as the gauze of clouds that had covered the moon came away, and what had been half in doubt was now unquestionably a nun. The hood she wore, like the *okoso* veils worn by women in later ages, covered her head and neck and fell to her shoulders, so that he could not make out her face from where he stood. Standing deject-edly and looking up at the sky, she was perhaps captivated by the blossoms, or drawn to the moon above them. . . . Quietly the nun came out from under the blossoms and started down the bluff. Arriving at the spring water, she leaned forward and reached for a branch of kerria.

As she did so, Shigemoto unconsciously stepped forward. Treading as softly as he could, he approached the nun from behind. She rose, holding the branch she had plucked, and started back up the bluff. Shigemoto could see now that a faint path traced its way uphill through the moss to a small, tottery gate, beyond which would be the nun's retreat.

"Excuse me . . ."

Startled at the sound of someone so near, the nun turned to face him. Shigemoto leaned forward, as if some force were pushing him from behind.

"Excuse me . . . Are you, by any chance, the mother of the late Lord Middle Counselor?" Shigemoto stammered.

"I was as you say, before I left the world. . . . And you?"

"I . . . I . . . I am the late Major Counselor's orphan, Shigemoto."

Then, as if a dam had burst, he suddenly cried, "Mother!" The nun staggered as the bulky man rushed up and threw his arms around her. With some difficulty she sat down on a rock at the side of the path.

"Mother," said Shigemoto again. Kneeling on the ground, he looked up at his mother and rested his head on her lap. Under the white hood her face was blurred by the light of the moon filtering through the cherry blossoms; sweet and small, it looked as though it were framed by a halo. The memory of that spring day forty years before, when he had been held in her arms behind a curtain stand, came vividly to life, and in an instant he felt as though he had become a child of five or six. In a reverie, he brushed aside the kerria branch she held and pressed his face closer to hers. The fragrance of incense in the sleeves of her black robe recalled to him that lingering scent of long ago, and like a child secure in his mother's love, he wiped his tears again and again with her sleeve.

TRANSLATOR'S ACKNOWLEDGMENTS

I wish to thank the National Endowment for the Arts, which provided support for the translation of *Captain Shigemoto's Mother*. Professors Robert Borgen, Lynne Miyake, Mildred Tahara, and Marian Ury provided valuable assistance and encouragement. Translations of court titles and other specialized terms follow those established by William H. and Helen Craig McCullough in *A Tale of Flowering Fortunes* (Stanford University Press, 1980). Professor Aileen Gatten applied her erudition in Heian literature and culture to an early draft of the translation and corrected a great many errors. Any that remain are, of course, my responsibility. Edward Seidensticker's translations of Tanizaki, including an excerpt from *Shigemoto*, have been inspirational. The late Tanizaki Matsuko, who told me that she loved *Captain Shigemoto's Mother* best among her husband's works, was a constant source of friendship and encouragement. My greatest debt is to my father, whose companionship and encouragement helped make the project possible and enjoyable.

English translations of many of Tanizaki's sources have lightened my task and make Tanizaki's neoclassical fiction more accessible to readers of English. The most important is Edward Seidensticker's translation of *The Tale of Genji*: the *Genji* is a constant, if usually implicit, presence in *The Reed Cutter* and *Captain Shigemoto's Mother*. Others include Susan Downing Videen's *Tales of Heichū*, Marian Ury's *Tales of Times Now Past*, Mildred Tahara's *Tales of Yamato*, and Helen Craig McCullough's *Ōkagami*.

—A.H.C.

Junichirō Tanizaki was born in 1886 in Tokyo, where his family owned a printing establishment. He studied Japanese literature at Tokyo Imperial University, and his first published work, a one-act play, appeared in 1910 in a literary magazine he helped to found.

Tanizaki lived in the cosmopolitan Tokyo area until the earthquake of 1923, when he moved to the gentler and more cultivated Kyoto-Osaka region, the scene of his great novel *The Makioka Sisters* (1943–48). There he became absorbed in the Japanese past and abandoned the more superficial aspects of his Westernization. His most important novels were written after 1923, among them—in addition to *The Makioka Sisters*—*Naomi* (1924), *Some Prefer Nettles* (1929), *Quicksand* (1930), *Arrowroot* (1931), *A Portrait of Shunkin* (1933), *The Secret History of the Lord of Musashi* (1935), modern versions of *The Tale of Genji* (1941, 1954, and 1965), *The Key* (1956), and *Diary of a Mad Old Man* (1961). He published *The Reed Cutter* in 1932 and *Captain Shigemoto's Mother* in 1949–50. By 1930 he had gained such renown that an edition of his complete works was published, and he received the Imperial Prize in Literature in 1949. Tanizaki died in 1965.

A NOTE ABOUT
THE TRANSLATOR

Anthony H. Chambers was born in Pasadena, California. He received his B.A. from Pomona College, his M.A. from Stanford University, and his Ph.D. in Japanese literature from the University of Michigan. He is Professor of Asian Languages and Literatures at Wesleyan University, and the translator of Tanizaki's novellas *The Secret History of the Lord of Musashi* and *Arrowroot*, and his novel *Naomi*.

A NOTE ON THE TYPE

This book was set in a digitized version of Janson. The hot-metal version of Janson was a recutting made direct from type cast from matrices long thought to have been made by the Dutchman Anton Janson, who was a practicing type founder in Leipzig during the years 1668–1687. However, it has been conclusively demonstrated that these types are actually the work of Nicholas Kis (1650–1702), a Hungarian, who most probably learned his trade from the master Dutch type founder Dirk Voskens. The type is an excellent example of the influential and sturdy Dutch types that prevailed in England up to the time William Caslon (1692–1766) developed his own incomparable designs from them.

Composed by ComCom, a division of Haddon Craftsmen, Allentown, Pennsylvania
Printed and bound by The Haddon Craftsmen, Scranton, Pennsylvania
Typography and binding design by Iris Weinstein